CHICAGOLAND DETECTIVE AGENCY

Nº6

A Midterm Night's Scheme

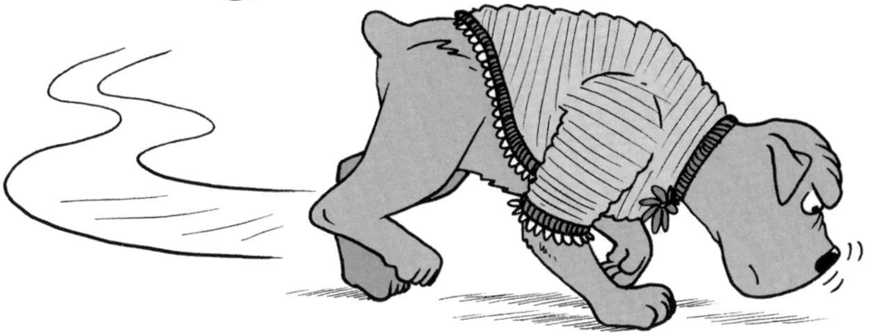

TRINA ROBBINS

ILLUSTRATED BY TYLER PAGE

GRAPHIC UNIVERSE™ • MINNEAPOLIS

STORY BY **TRINA ROBBINS**
PENCILS AND INKS BY **TYLER PAGE**
LETTERING BY **ZACK GIALLONGO**
COVER COLORING BY **HI-FI DESIGN**

Graphic Universe™
A division of Lerner Publishing Group, Inc.
241 First Avenue North
Minneapolis, MN 55401 USA

For reading levels and more information, look up this title at www.lernerbooks.com.

Main body text set in CC Wild Words.
Typeface provided by Comicraft Design.

Library of Congress Cataloging-in-Publication Data

Robbins, Trina.
    A midterm night's scheme / by Trina Robbins ; illustrated by Tyler Page.
        p. cm. — (Chicagoland Detective Agency ; #06)
    Summary: Megan's new friend Luna has a mystery for the Chicagoland Detective Agency to solve: who's been following her and stealing the notes for her science fair experiment? Luna's experiment is all about potions.
    ISBN 978-0-7613-8167-9 (lib. bdg. : alk. paper)
    ISBN 978-1-4677-1635-2 (eBook)
    1. Graphic novels. [1. Graphic novels. 2. Mystery and detective stories.
3. Science—Experiments—Fiction. 4. Chicago (Ill.)—Fiction.] I. Page, Tyler, 1976– illustrator. II. Title.
PZ7.7.R632Mi 2014
741.5'973—dc23   2012047635

Manufactured in the United States of America
1 – BP – 12/31/13

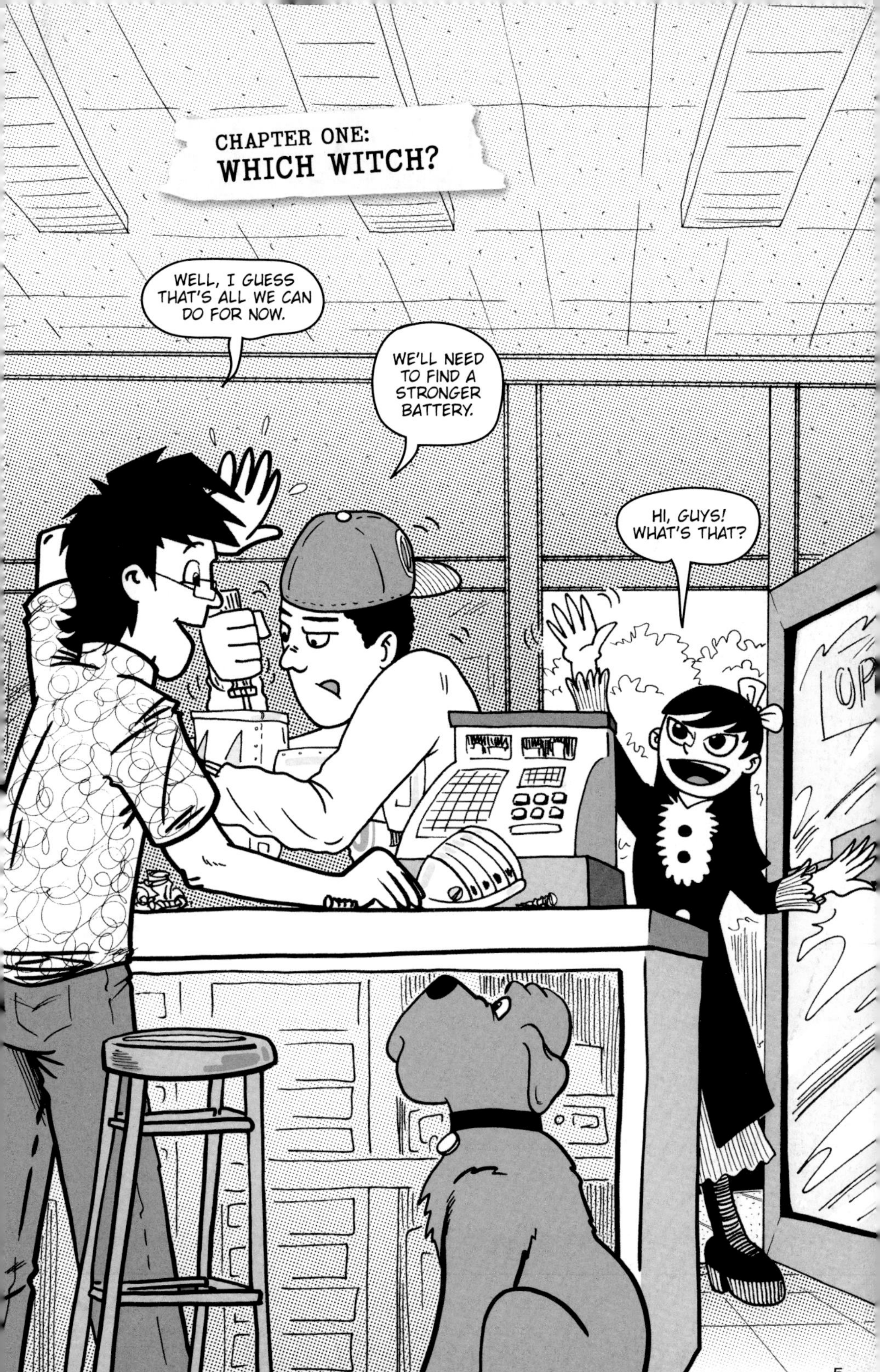
CHAPTER ONE:
WHICH WITCH?
WELL, I GUESS THAT'S ALL WE CAN DO FOR NOW.
WE'LL NEED TO FIND A STRONGER BATTERY.
HI, GUYS! WHAT'S THAT?

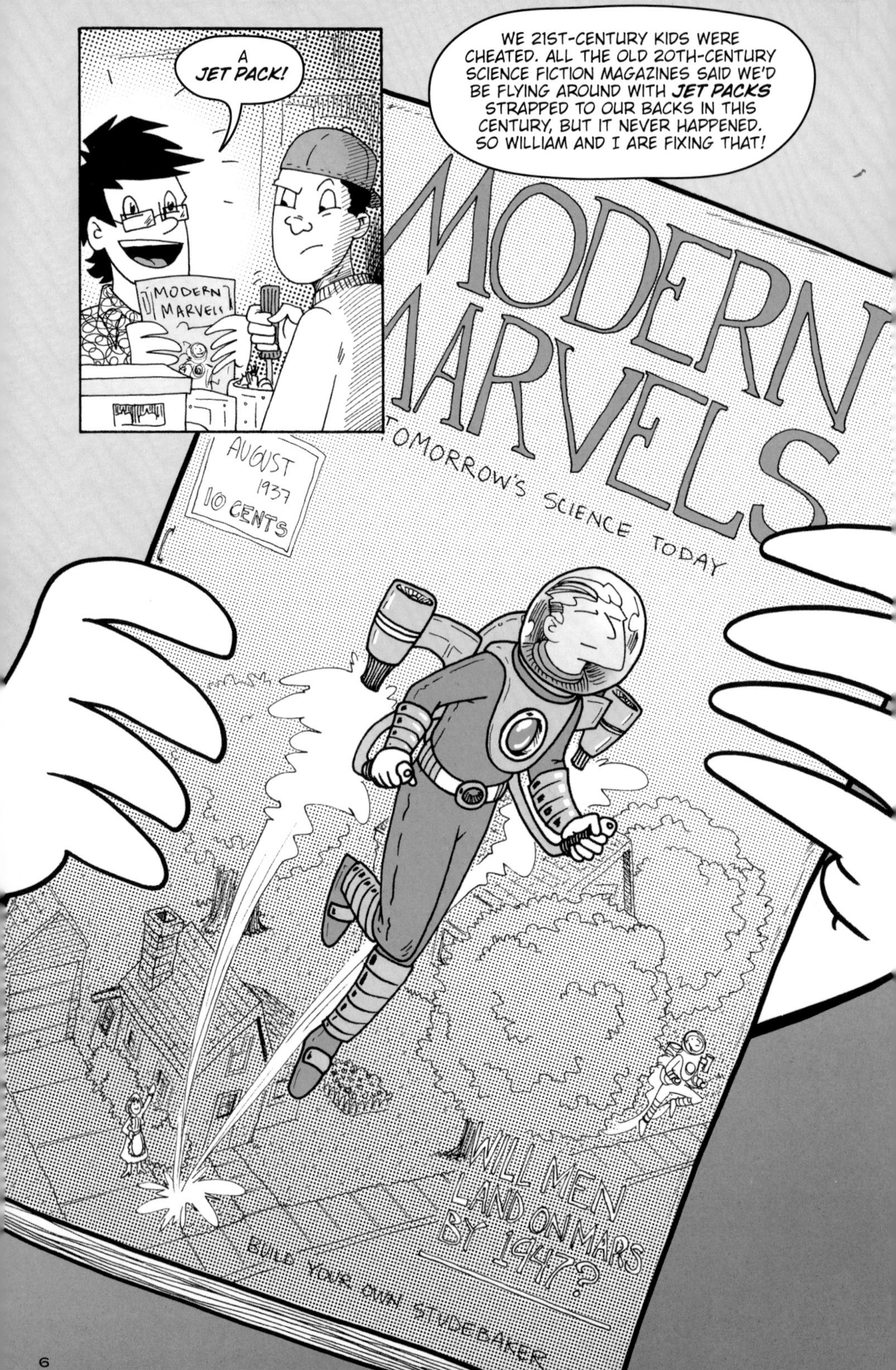

A JET PACK!
MODERN MARVELS
WE 21ST-CENTURY KIDS WERE CHEATED. ALL THE OLD 20TH-CENTURY SCIENCE FICTION MAGAZINES SAID WE'D BE FLYING AROUND WITH JET PACKS STRAPPED TO OUR BACKS IN THIS CENTURY, BUT IT NEVER HAPPENED. SO WILLIAM AND I ARE FIXING THAT!
MODERN MARVELS
TOMORROW'S SCIENCE TODAY
AUGUST 1937 10 CENTS
WILL MEN LAND ON MARS BY 1947?
BUILD YOUR OWN STUDEBAKER

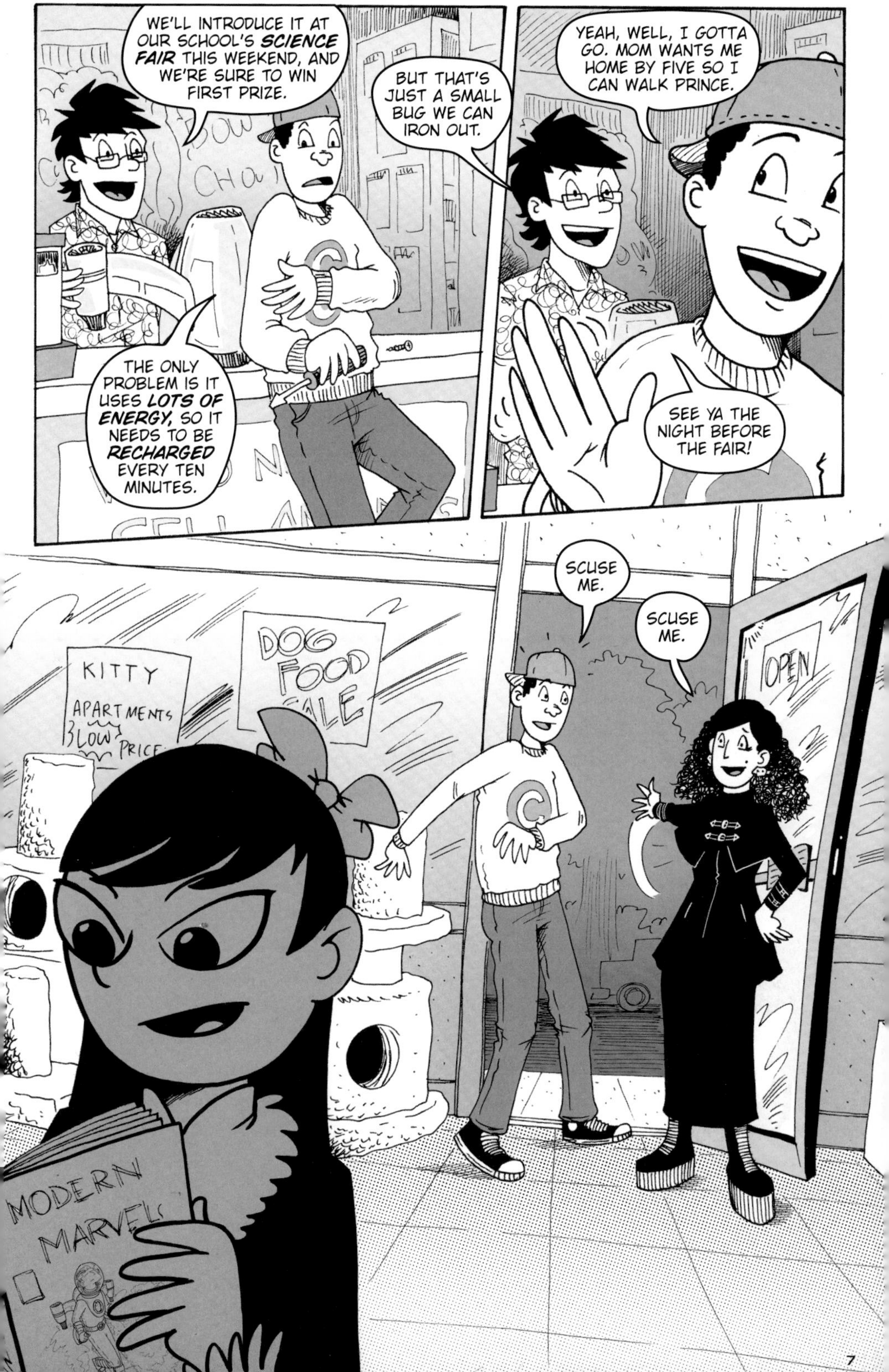

WE'LL INTRODUCE IT AT OUR SCHOOL'S SCIENCE FAIR THIS WEEKEND, AND WE'RE SURE TO WIN FIRST PRIZE.
THE ONLY PROBLEM IS IT USES LOTS OF ENERGY, SO IT NEEDS TO BE RECHARGED EVERY TEN MINUTES.
BUT THAT'S JUST A SMALL BUG WE CAN IRON OUT.
YEAH, WELL, I GOTTA GO. MOM WANTS ME HOME BY FIVE SO I CAN WALK PRINCE.
SEE YA THE NIGHT BEFORE THE FAIR!
KITTY APARTMENTS LOW PRICE
DOG FOOD SALE
SCUSE ME.
SCUSE ME.
OPEN
MODERN MARVELS

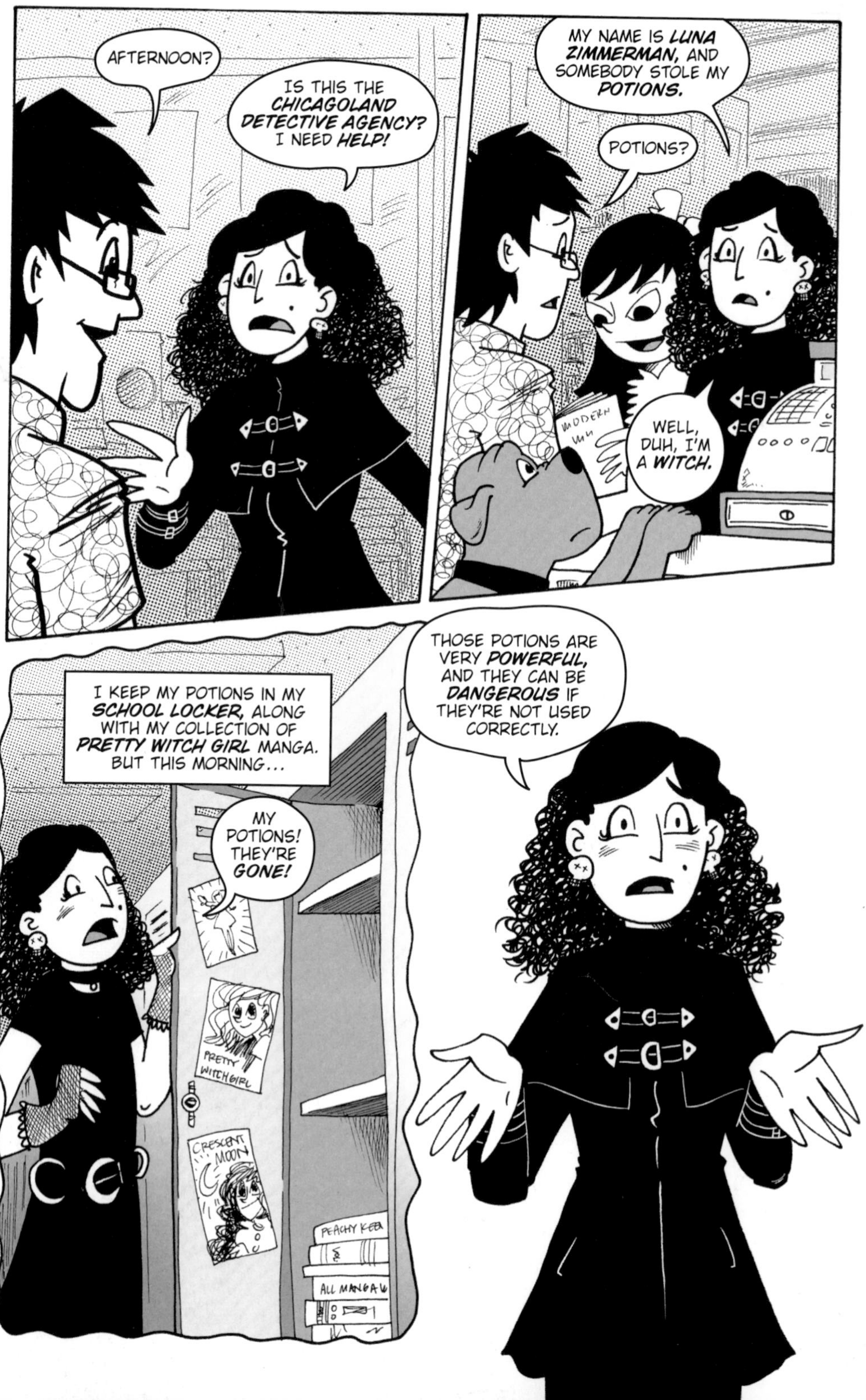
AFTERNOON?
IS THIS THE CHICAGOLAND DETECTIVE AGENCY? I NEED HELP!
MY NAME IS LUNA ZIMMERMAN, AND SOMEBODY STOLE MY POTIONS.
POTIONS?
MODERN
WELL, DUH, I'M A WITCH.
I KEEP MY POTIONS IN MY SCHOOL LOCKER, ALONG WITH MY COLLECTION OF PRETTY WITCH GIRL MANGA. BUT THIS MORNING...
MY POTIONS! THEY'RE GONE!
PRETTY WITCHGIRL
CRESCENT MOON
PEACHY KEEN
ALL MANGA
THOSE POTIONS ARE VERY POWERFUL, AND THEY CAN BE DANGEROUS IF THEY'RE NOT USED CORRECTLY.

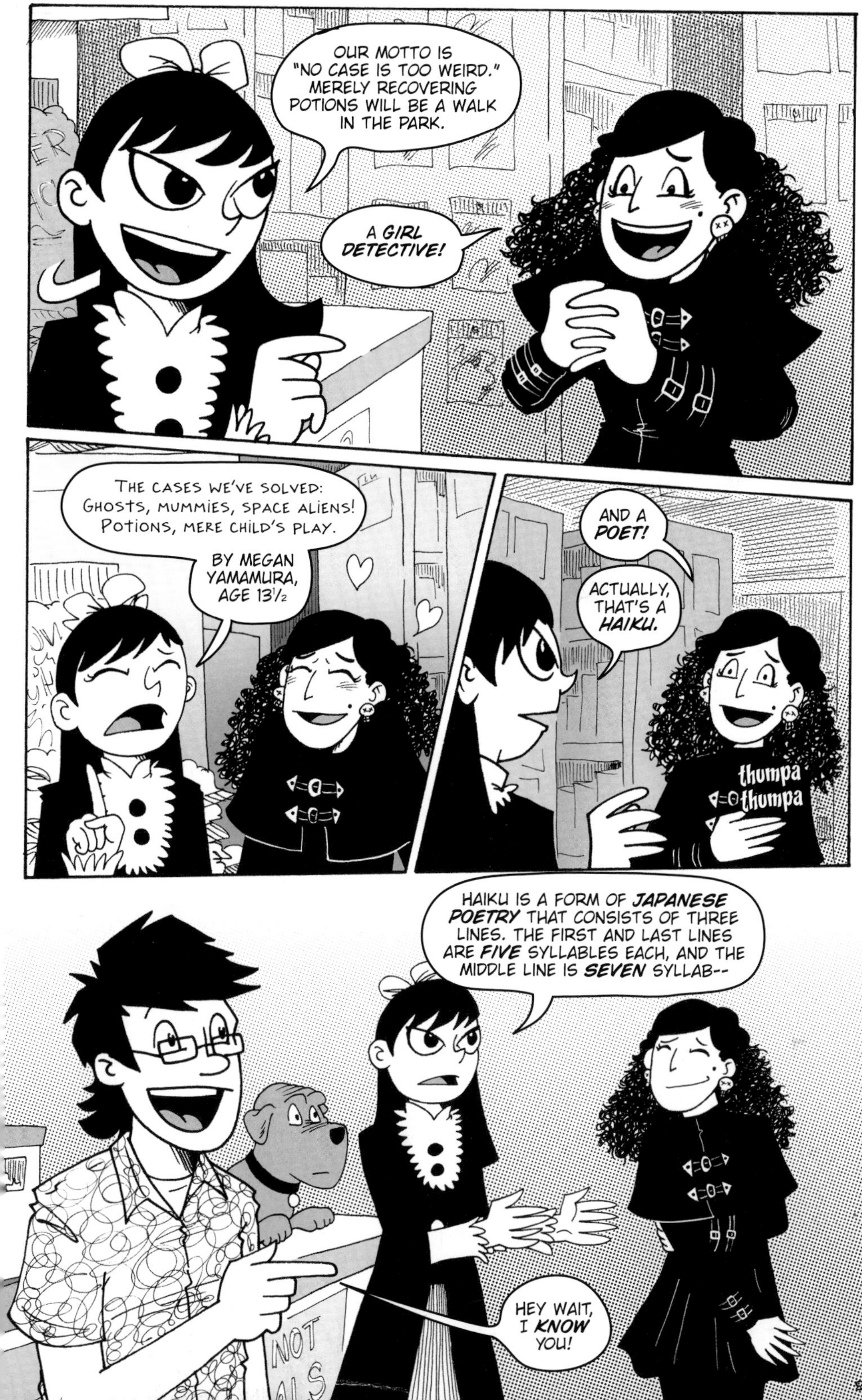

OUR MOTTO IS "NO CASE IS TOO WEIRD." MERELY RECOVERING POTIONS WILL BE A WALK IN THE PARK.
A GIRL DETECTIVE!
THE CASES WE'VE SOLVED: GHOSTS, MUMMIES, SPACE ALIENS! POTIONS, MERE CHILD'S PLAY.
BY MEGAN YAMAMURA, AGE 13½
AND A POET!
ACTUALLY, THAT'S A HAIKU.
thumpa thumpa
HAIKU IS A FORM OF JAPANESE POETRY THAT CONSISTS OF THREE LINES. THE FIRST AND LAST LINES ARE FIVE SYLLABLES EACH, AND THE MIDDLE LINE IS SEVEN SYLLAB--
HEY WAIT, I KNOW YOU!

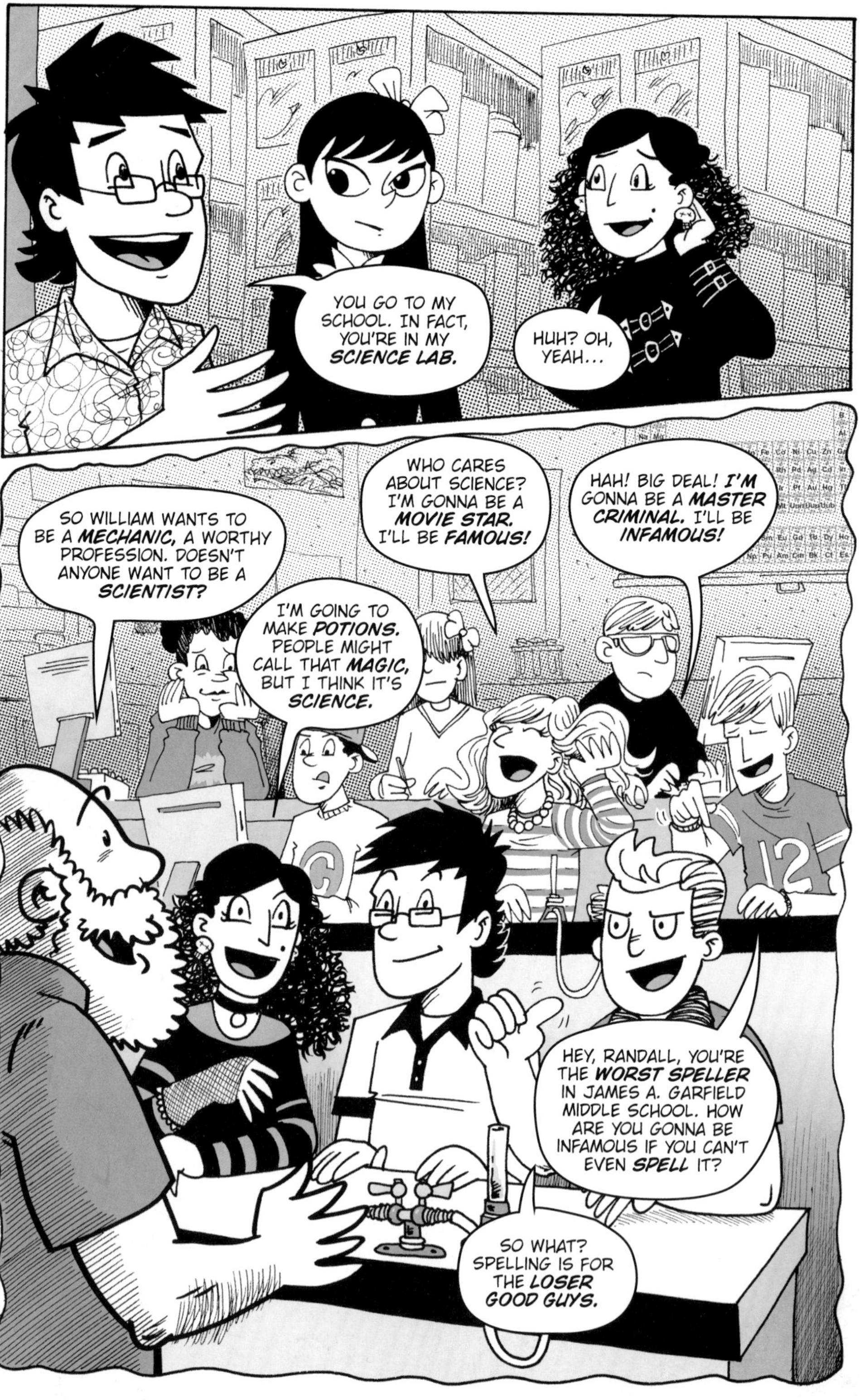
YOU GO TO MY SCHOOL. IN FACT, YOU'RE IN MY SCIENCE LAB.
HUH? OH, YEAH...
SO WILLIAM WANTS TO BE A MECHANIC, A WORTHY PROFESSION. DOESN'T ANYONE WANT TO BE A SCIENTIST?
I'M GOING TO MAKE POTIONS. PEOPLE MIGHT CALL THAT MAGIC, BUT I THINK IT'S SCIENCE.
WHO CARES ABOUT SCIENCE? I'M GONNA BE A MOVIE STAR. I'LL BE FAMOUS!
HAH! BIG DEAL! I'M GONNA BE A MASTER CRIMINAL. I'LL BE INFAMOUS!
HEY, RANDALL, YOU'RE THE WORST SPELLER IN JAMES A. GARFIELD MIDDLE SCHOOL. HOW ARE YOU GONNA BE INFAMOUS IF YOU CAN'T EVEN SPELL IT?
SO WHAT? SPELLING IS FOR THE LOSER GOOD GUYS.

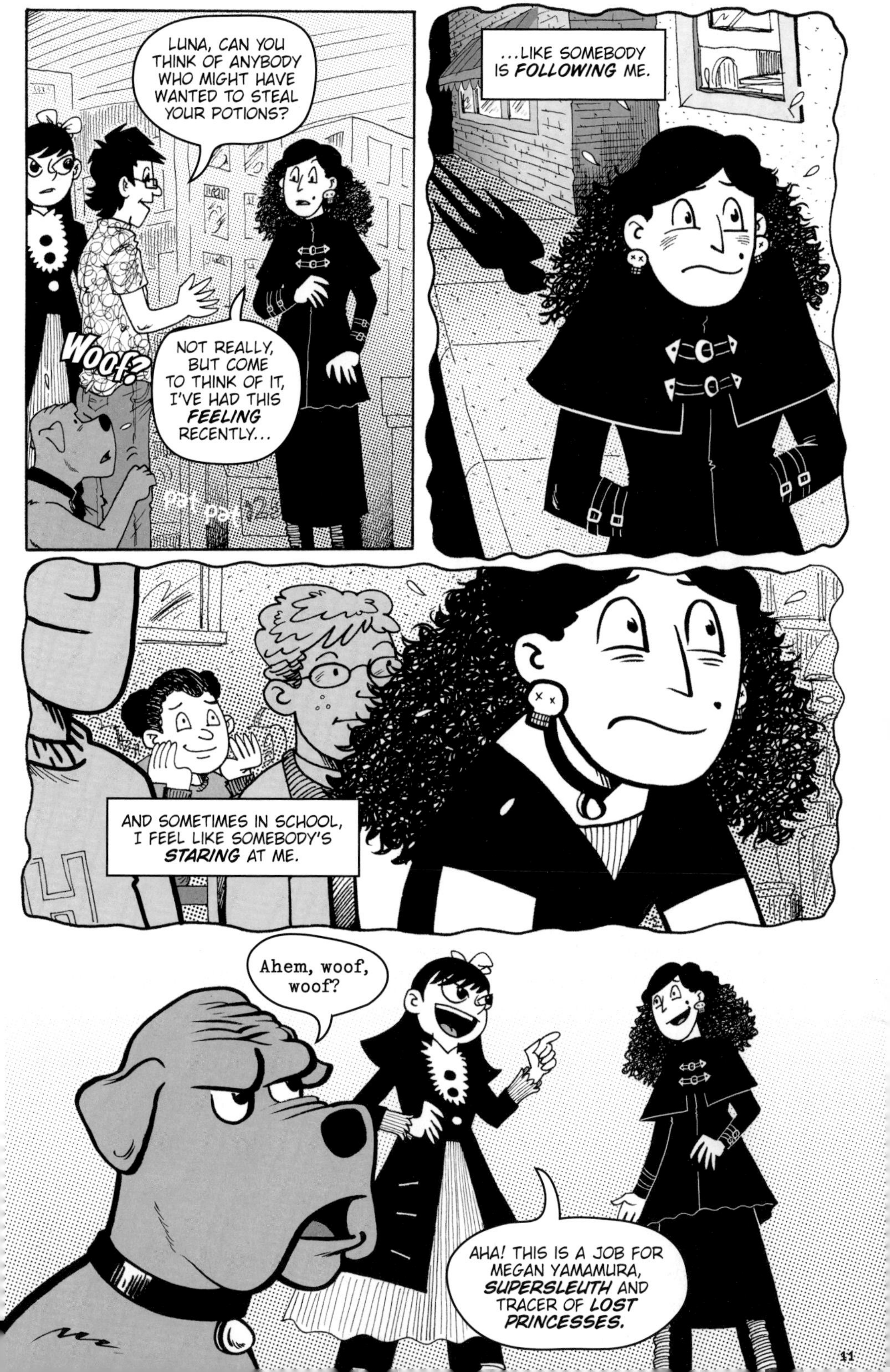

LUNA, CAN YOU THINK OF ANYBODY WHO MIGHT HAVE WANTED TO STEAL YOUR POTIONS?
WOOF?
NOT REALLY, BUT COME TO THINK OF IT, I'VE HAD THIS FEELING RECENTLY...
pat pat
...LIKE SOMEBODY IS FOLLOWING ME.
AND SOMETIMES IN SCHOOL, I FEEL LIKE SOMEBODY'S STARING AT ME.
Ahem, woof, woof?
AHA! THIS IS A JOB FOR MEGAN YAMAMURA, SUPERSLEUTH AND TRACER OF LOST PRINCESSES.

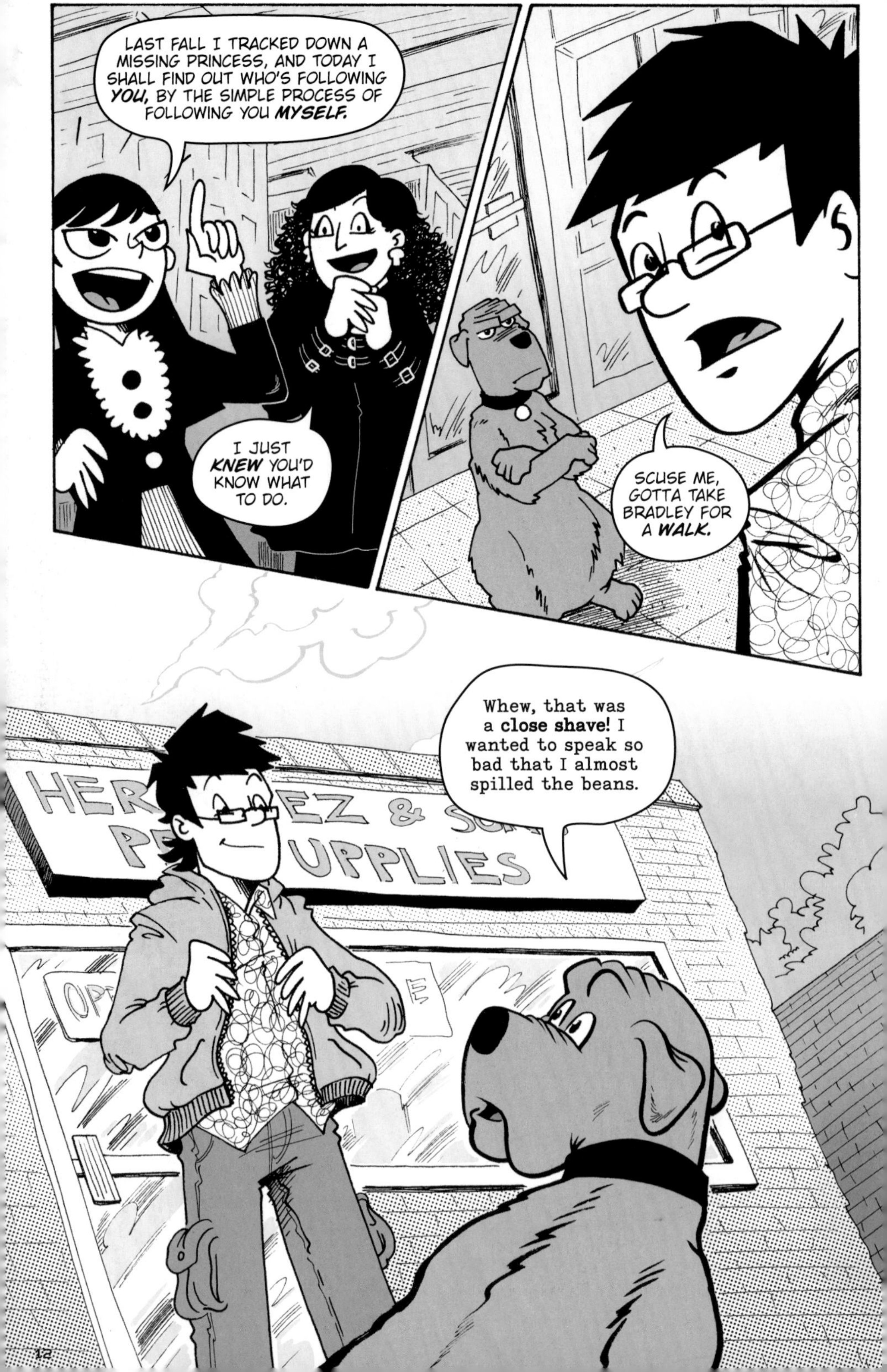

LAST FALL I TRACKED DOWN A MISSING PRINCESS, AND TODAY I SHALL FIND OUT WHO'S FOLLOWING YOU, BY THE SIMPLE PROCESS OF FOLLOWING YOU MYSELF.
I JUST KNEW YOU'D KNOW WHAT TO DO.
SCUSE ME, GOTTA TAKE BRADLEY FOR A WALK.
Whew, that was a close shave! I wanted to speak so bad that I almost spilled the beans.

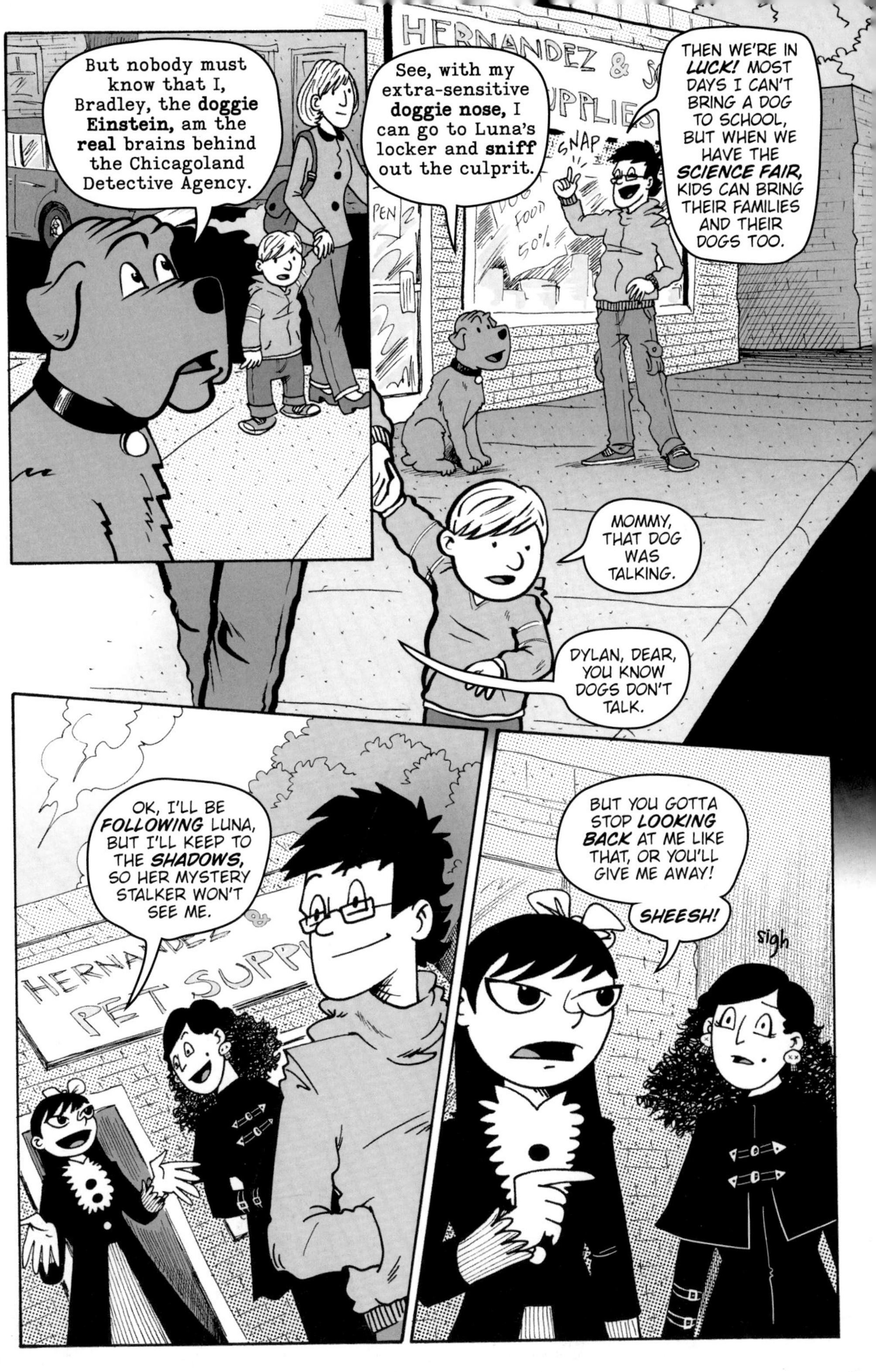
But nobody must know that I, Bradley, the doggie Einstein, am the real brains behind the Chicagoland Detective Agency.
See, with my extra-sensitive doggie nose, I can go to Luna's locker and sniff out the culprit.
HERNANDEZ & S... SUPPLIES
SNAP
THEN WE'RE IN LUCK! MOST DAYS I CAN'T BRING A DOG TO SCHOOL, BUT WHEN WE HAVE THE SCIENCE FAIR, KIDS CAN BRING THEIR FAMILIES AND THEIR DOGS TOO.
MOMMY, THAT DOG WAS TALKING.
DYLAN, DEAR, YOU KNOW DOGS DON'T TALK.
OK, I'LL BE FOLLOWING LUNA, BUT I'LL KEEP TO THE SHADOWS, SO HER MYSTERY STALKER WON'T SEE ME.
BUT YOU GOTTA STOP LOOKING BACK AT ME LIKE THAT, OR YOU'LL GIVE ME AWAY!
SHEESH!
sigh

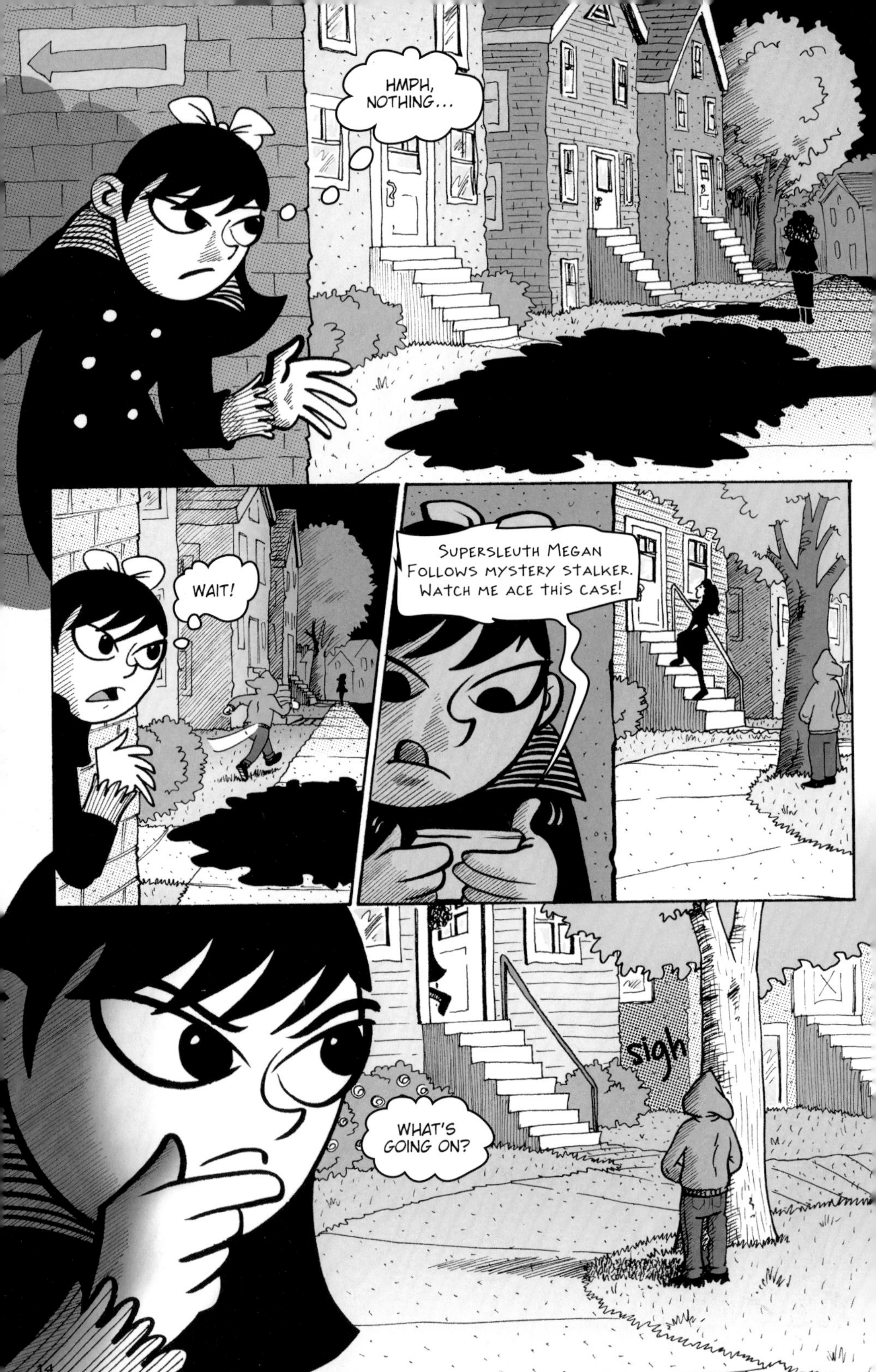
HMPH, NOTHING...
WAIT!
SUPERSLEUTH MEGAN FOLLOWS MYSTERY STALKER. WATCH ME ACE THIS CASE!
sigh
WHAT'S GOING ON?

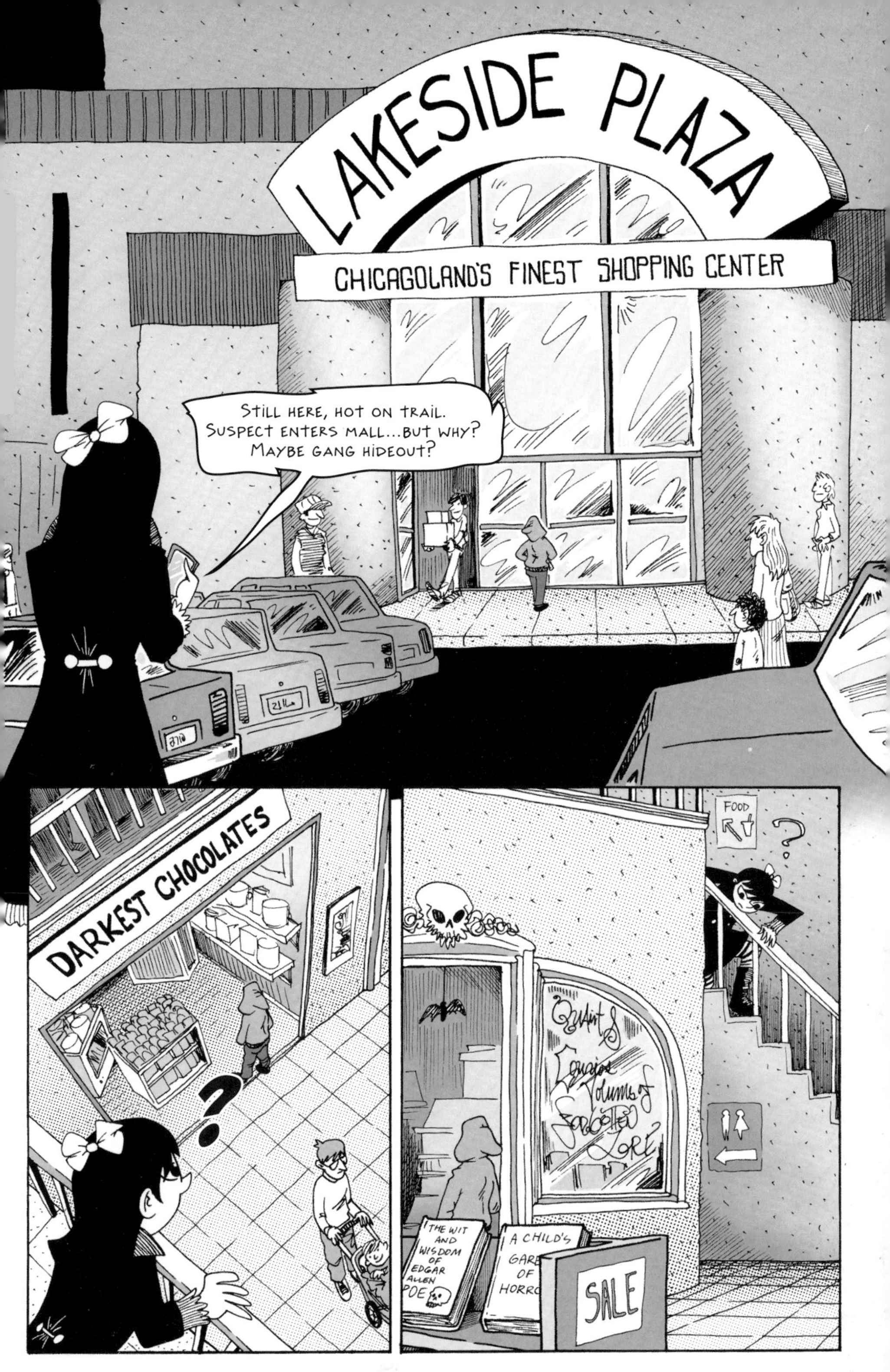
LAKESIDE PLAZA
CHICAGOLAND'S FINEST SHOPPING CENTER
STILL HERE, HOT ON TRAIL. SUSPECT ENTERS MALL...BUT WHY? MAYBE GANG HIDEOUT?
DARKEST CHOCOLATES
FOOD
Quaint & Curious Volumes of Forgotten Lore
THE WIT AND WISDOM OF EDGAR ALLEN POE
A CHILD'S GARE OF HORRO
SALE

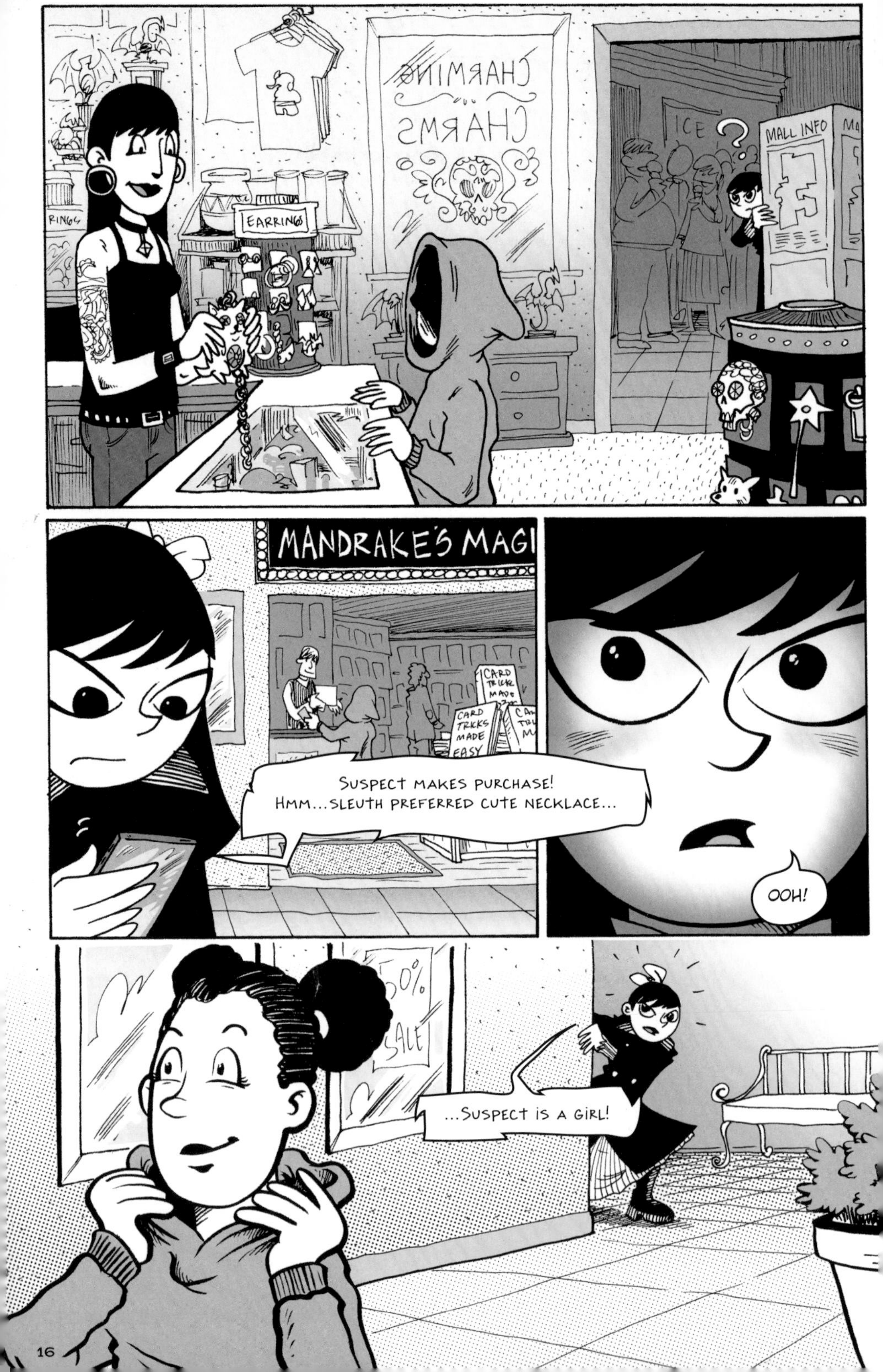
CHARMING CHARMS
RINGS
EARRINGS
ICE
MALL INFO
MANDRAKE'S MAGI
CARD TRICKS MADE EASY
SUSPECT MAKES PURCHASE! HMM...SLEUTH PREFERRED CUTE NECKLACE...
OOH!
SALE
...SUSPECT IS A GIRL!

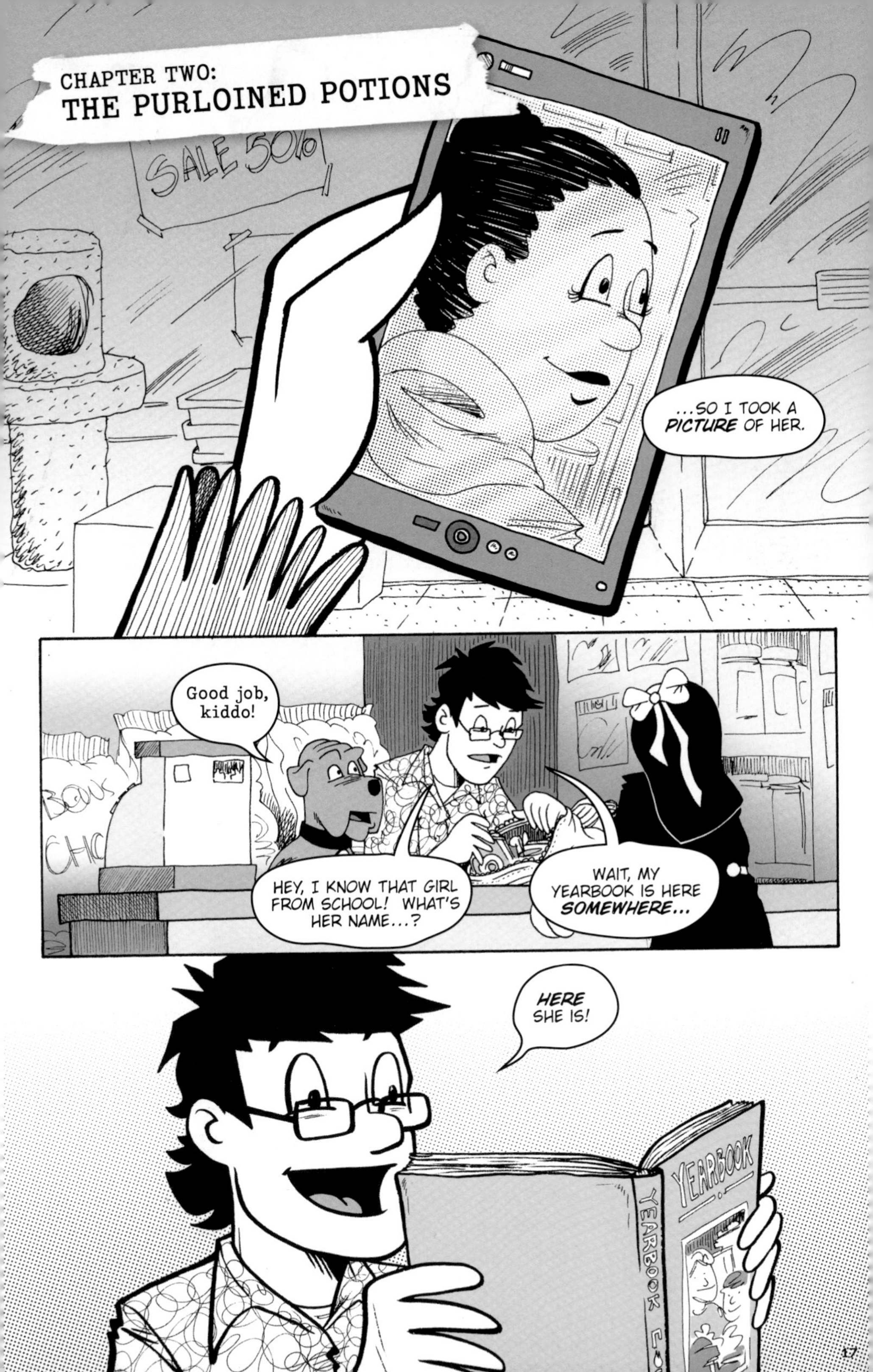
CHAPTER TWO:
THE PURLOINED POTIONS
SALE 50%
...SO I TOOK A PICTURE OF HER.
Good job, kiddo!
HEY, I KNOW THAT GIRL FROM SCHOOL! WHAT'S HER NAME...?
WAIT, MY YEARBOOK IS HERE SOMEWHERE...
HERE SHE IS!
YEARBOOK
YEARBOOK

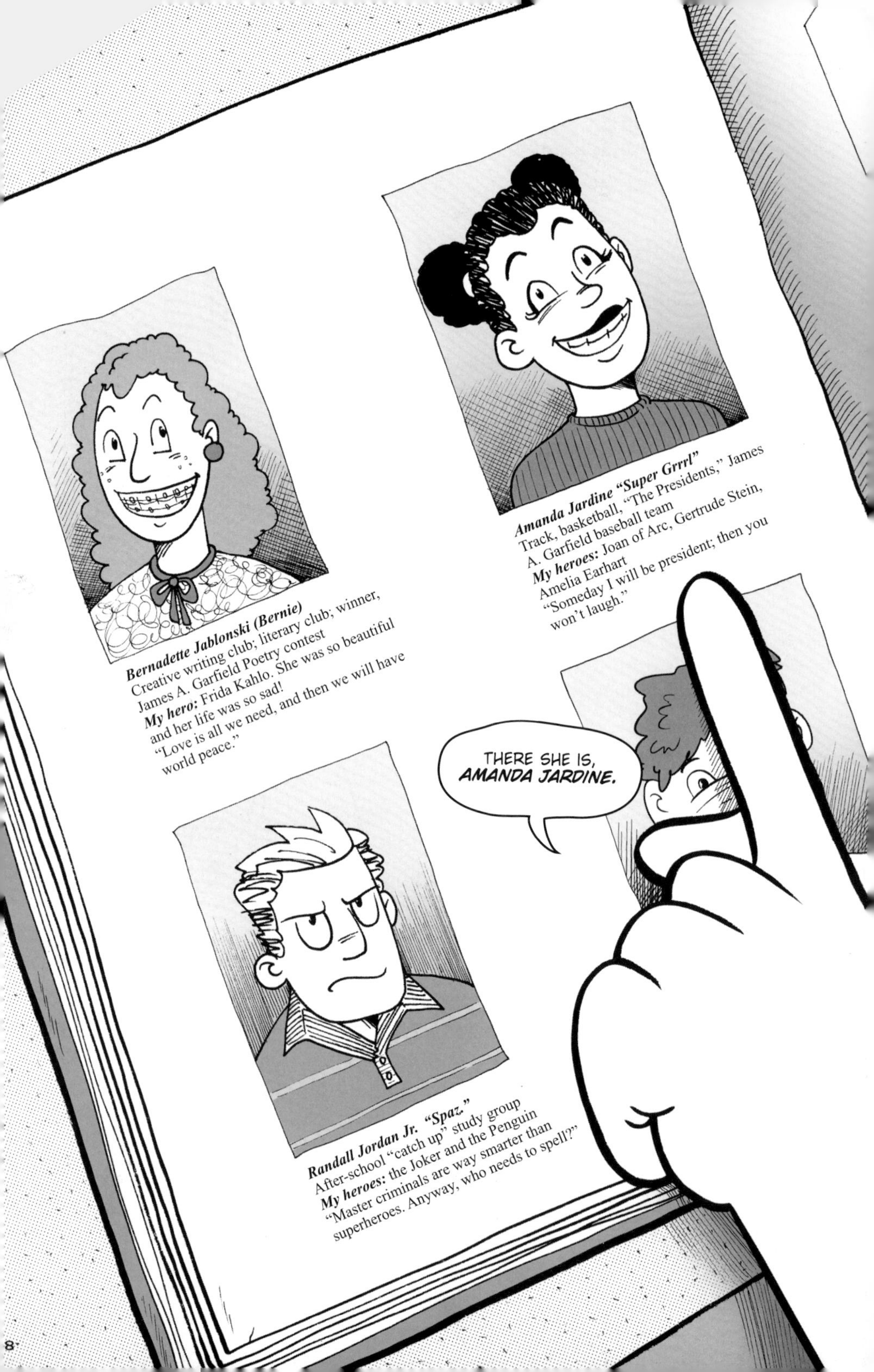

Bernadette Jablonski (Bernie)
Creative writing club; literary club; winner, James A. Garfield Poetry contest
My hero: Frida Kahlo. She was so beautiful and her life was so sad!
"Love is all we need, and then we will have world peace."
Amanda Jardine "Super Grrrl"
Track, basketball, "The Presidents," James A. Garfield baseball team
My heroes: Joan of Arc, Gertrude Stein, Amelia Earhart
"Someday I will be president; then you won't laugh."
THERE SHE IS, AMANDA JARDINE.
Randall Jordan Jr. "Spaz."
After-school "catch up" study group
My heroes: the Joker and the Penguin
"Master criminals are way smarter than superheroes. Anyway, who needs to spell?"

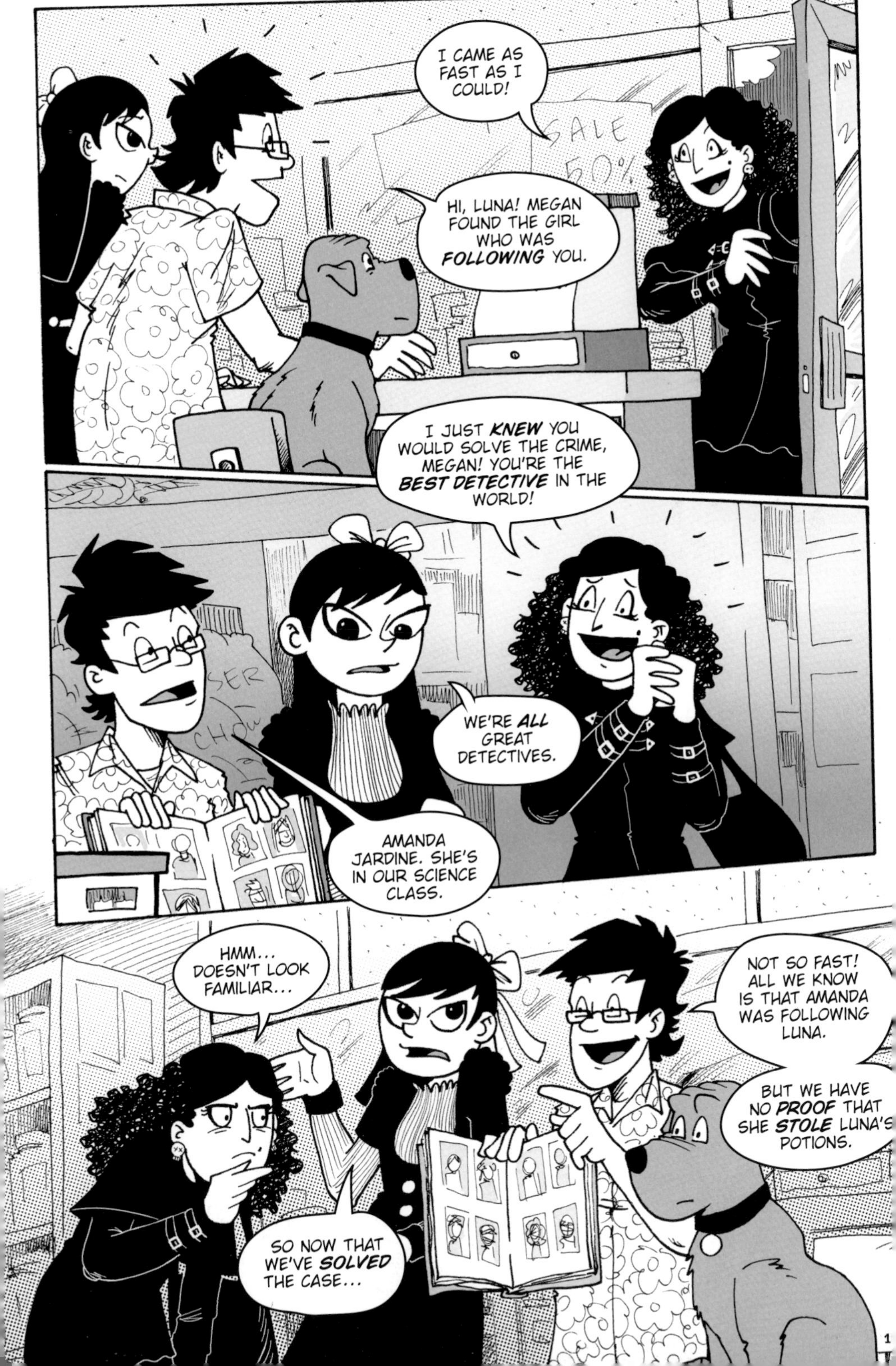
I CAME AS FAST AS I COULD!
HI, LUNA! MEGAN FOUND THE GIRL WHO WAS FOLLOWING YOU.
I JUST KNEW YOU WOULD SOLVE THE CRIME, MEGAN! YOU'RE THE BEST DETECTIVE IN THE WORLD!
WE'RE ALL GREAT DETECTIVES.
AMANDA JARDINE. SHE'S IN OUR SCIENCE CLASS.
HMM... DOESN'T LOOK FAMILIAR...
SO NOW THAT WE'VE SOLVED THE CASE...
NOT SO FAST! ALL WE KNOW IS THAT AMANDA WAS FOLLOWING LUNA.
BUT WE HAVE NO PROOF THAT SHE STOLE LUNA'S POTIONS.

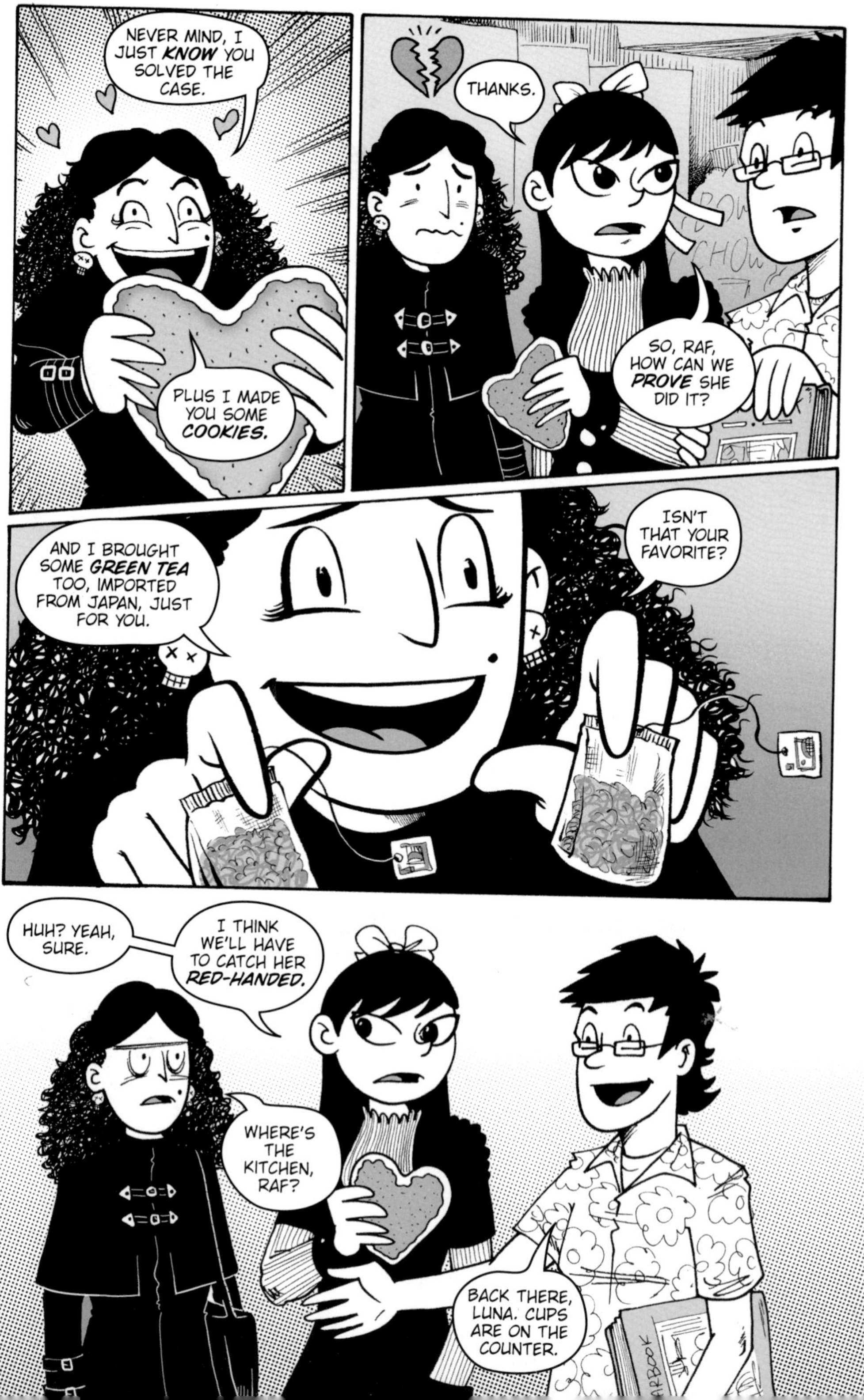
NEVER MIND, I JUST KNOW YOU SOLVED THE CASE.
PLUS I MADE YOU SOME COOKIES.
THANKS.
SO, RAF, HOW CAN WE PROVE SHE DID IT?
AND I BROUGHT SOME GREEN TEA TOO, IMPORTED FROM JAPAN, JUST FOR YOU.
ISN'T THAT YOUR FAVORITE?
HUH? YEAH, SURE.
I THINK WE'LL HAVE TO CATCH HER RED-HANDED.
WHERE'S THE KITCHEN, RAF?
BACK THERE, LUNA. CUPS ARE ON THE COUNTER.

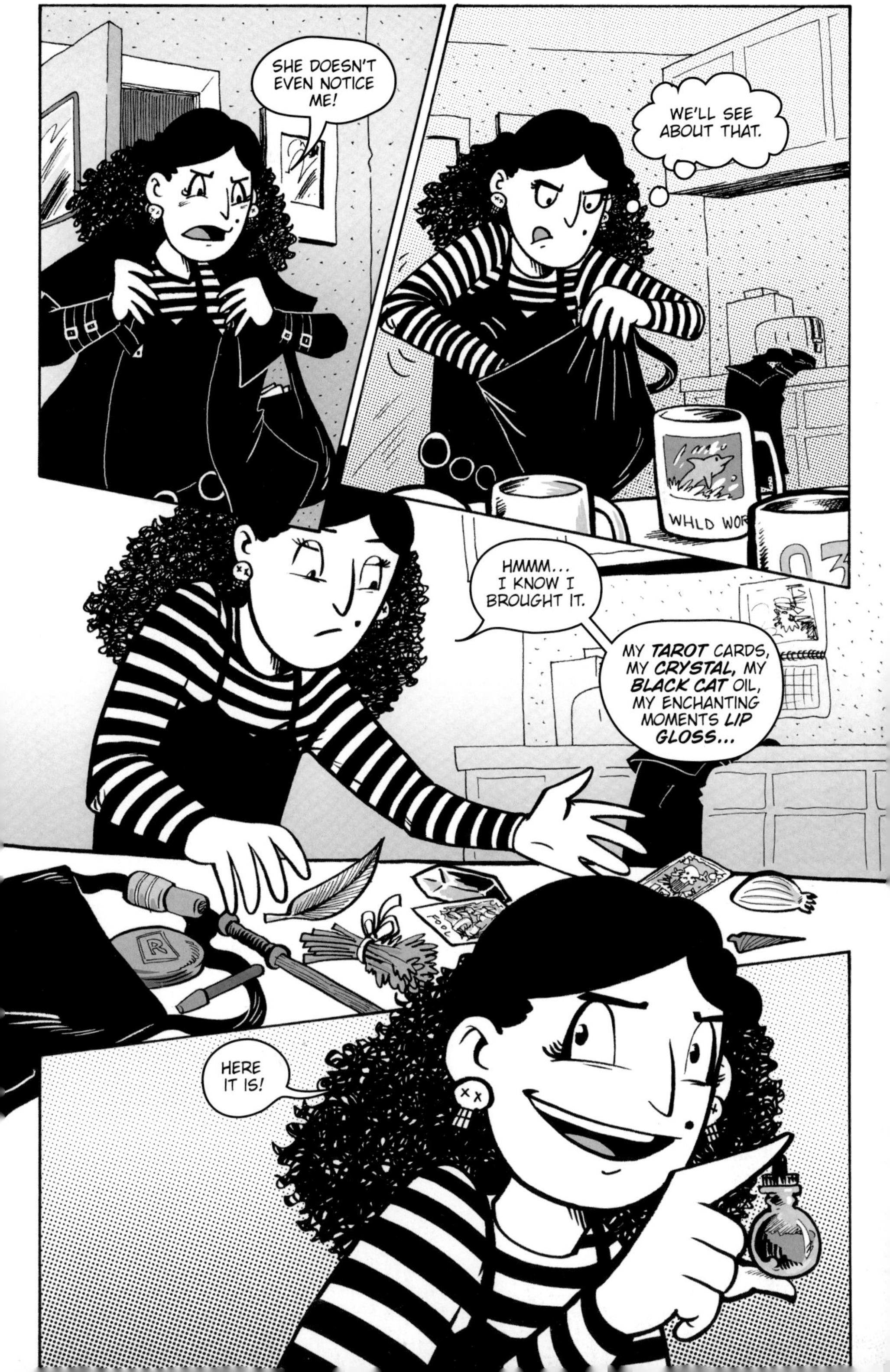
SHE DOESN'T EVEN NOTICE ME!
WE'LL SEE ABOUT THAT.
WHLD WOR
HMMM... I KNOW I BROUGHT IT.
MY TAROT CARDS, MY CRYSTAL, MY BLACK CAT OIL, MY ENCHANTING MOMENTS LIP GLOSS...
FOOL
HERE IT IS!

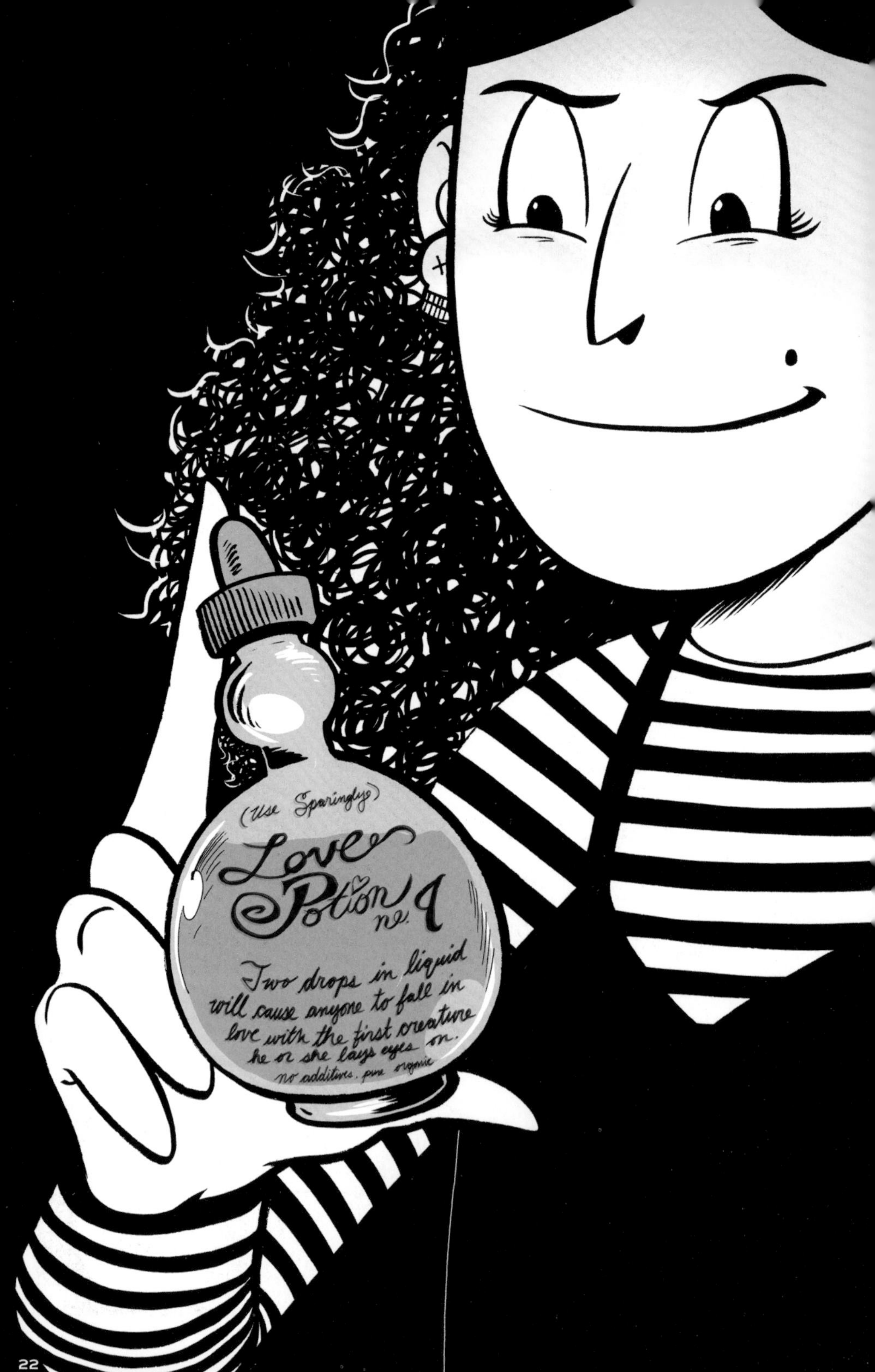
(Use Sparingly)
Love Potion no. 9
Two drops in liquid will cause anyone to fall in love with the first creature he or she lays eyes on.
no additives. pure organic

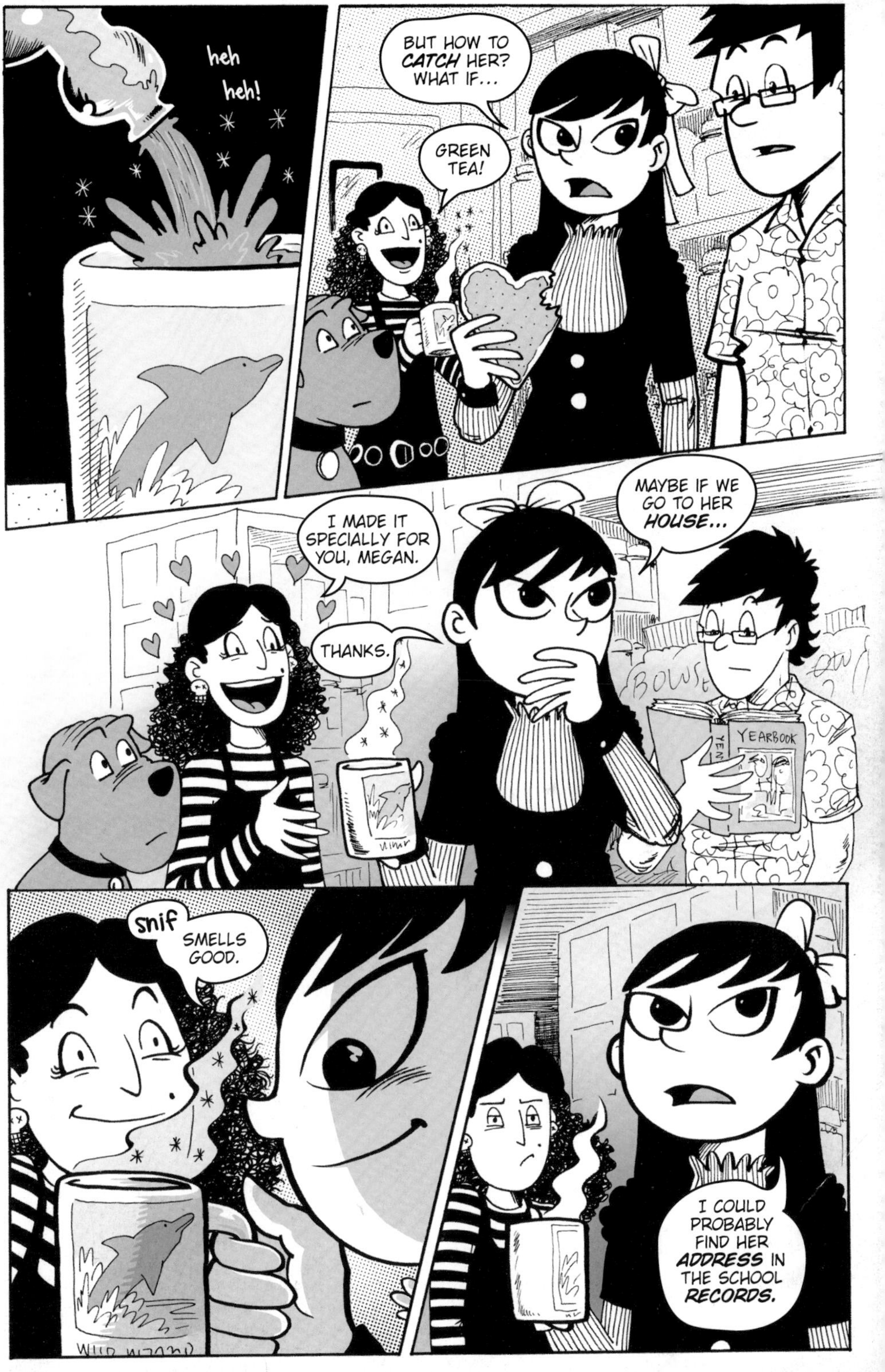
heh
heh!
BUT HOW TO CATCH HER? WHAT IF...
GREEN TEA!
I MADE IT SPECIALLY FOR YOU, MEGAN.
MAYBE IF WE GO TO HER HOUSE...
THANKS.
YEARBOOK
snif
SMELLS GOOD.
I COULD PROBABLY FIND HER ADDRESS IN THE SCHOOL RECORDS.

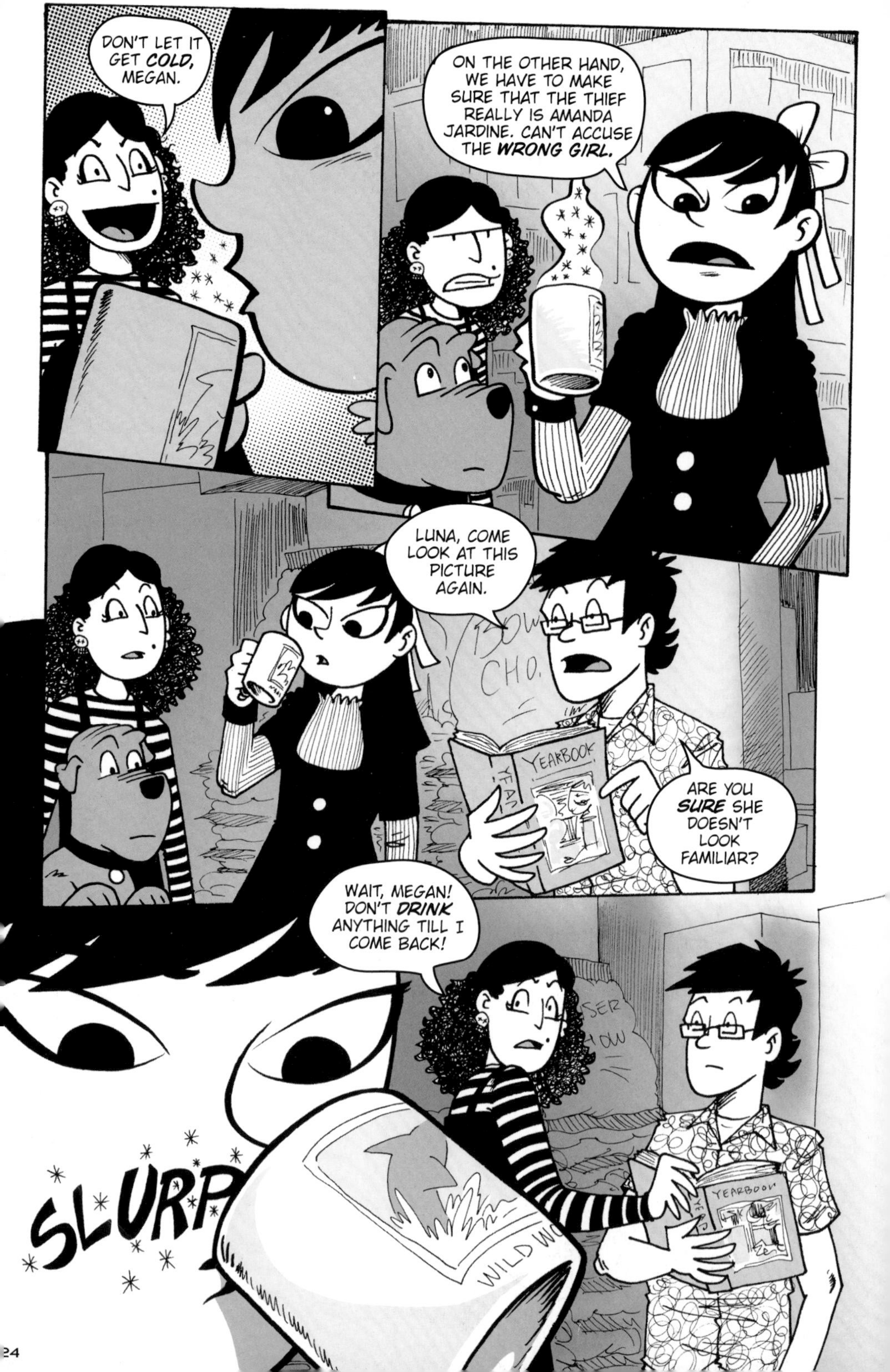
DON'T LET IT GET COLD, MEGAN.
ON THE OTHER HAND, WE HAVE TO MAKE SURE THAT THE THIEF REALLY IS AMANDA JARDINE. CAN'T ACCUSE THE WRONG GIRL.
LUNA, COME LOOK AT THIS PICTURE AGAIN.
YEARBOOK
ARE YOU SURE SHE DOESN'T LOOK FAMILIAR?
WAIT, MEGAN! DON'T DRINK ANYTHING TILL I COME BACK!
SLURP
YEARBOOK

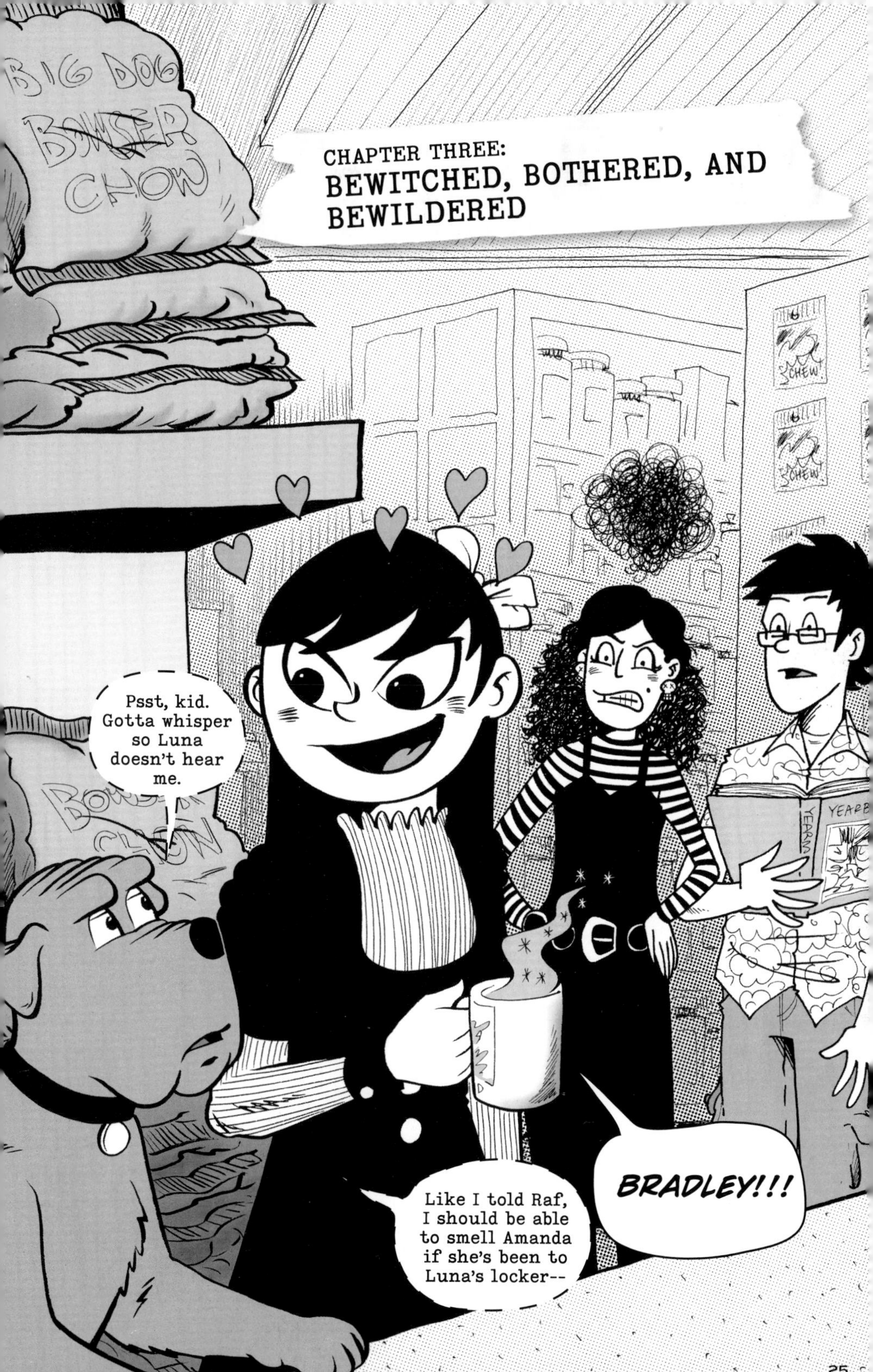
BIG DOG
BOWSER
CHOW
CHAPTER THREE:
BEWITCHED, BOTHERED, AND BEWILDERED
Psst, kid. Gotta whisper so Luna doesn't hear me.
Like I told Raf, I should be able to smell Amanda if she's been to Luna's locker--
BRADLEY!!!
CHEW
CHEW

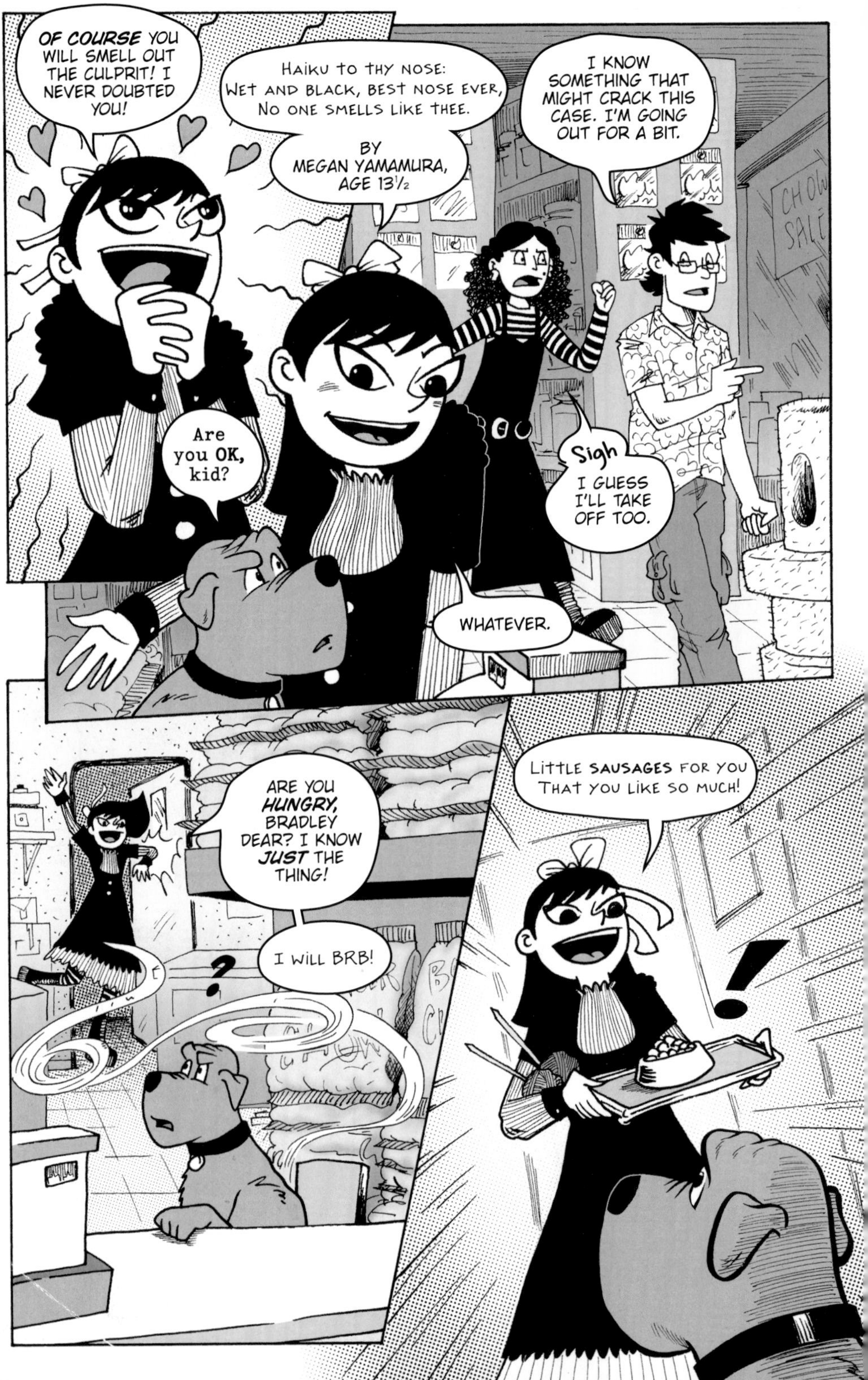

OF COURSE YOU WILL SMELL OUT THE CULPRIT! I NEVER DOUBTED YOU!
Haiku to thy nose: Wet and black, best nose ever, No one smells like thee.
BY MEGAN YAMAMURA, AGE 13½
I KNOW SOMETHING THAT MIGHT CRACK THIS CASE. I'M GOING OUT FOR A BIT.
Are you OK, kid?
Sigh
I GUESS I'LL TAKE OFF TOO.
WHATEVER.
ARE YOU HUNGRY, BRADLEY DEAR? I KNOW JUST THE THING!
I will BRB!
Little SAUSAGES for you That you like so much!

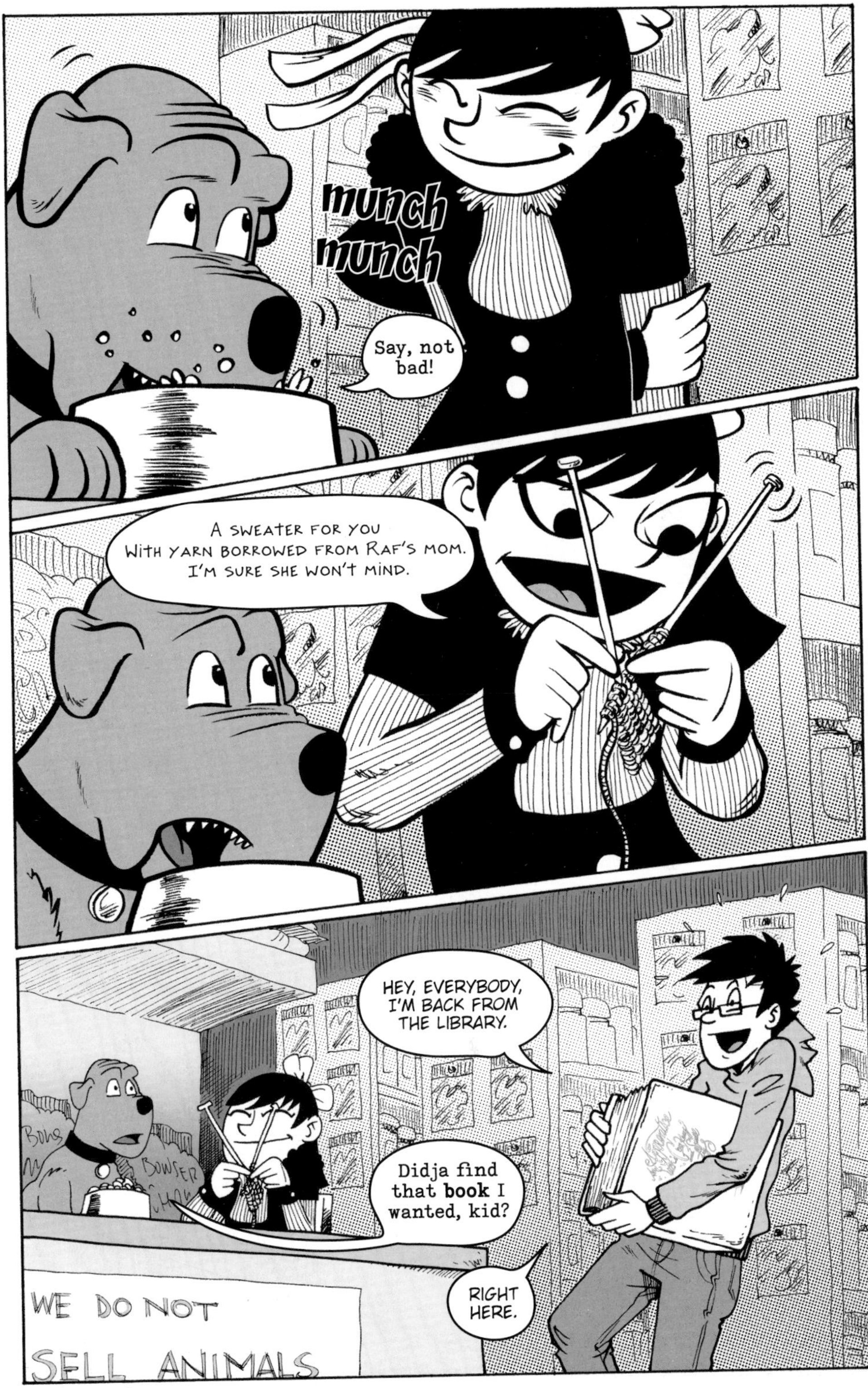
munch munch
Say, not bad!
A SWEATER FOR YOU WITH YARN BORROWED FROM RAF'S MOM. I'M SURE SHE WON'T MIND.
HEY, EVERYBODY, I'M BACK FROM THE LIBRARY.
Didja find that **book** I wanted, kid?
RIGHT HERE.
WE DO NOT SELL ANIMALS

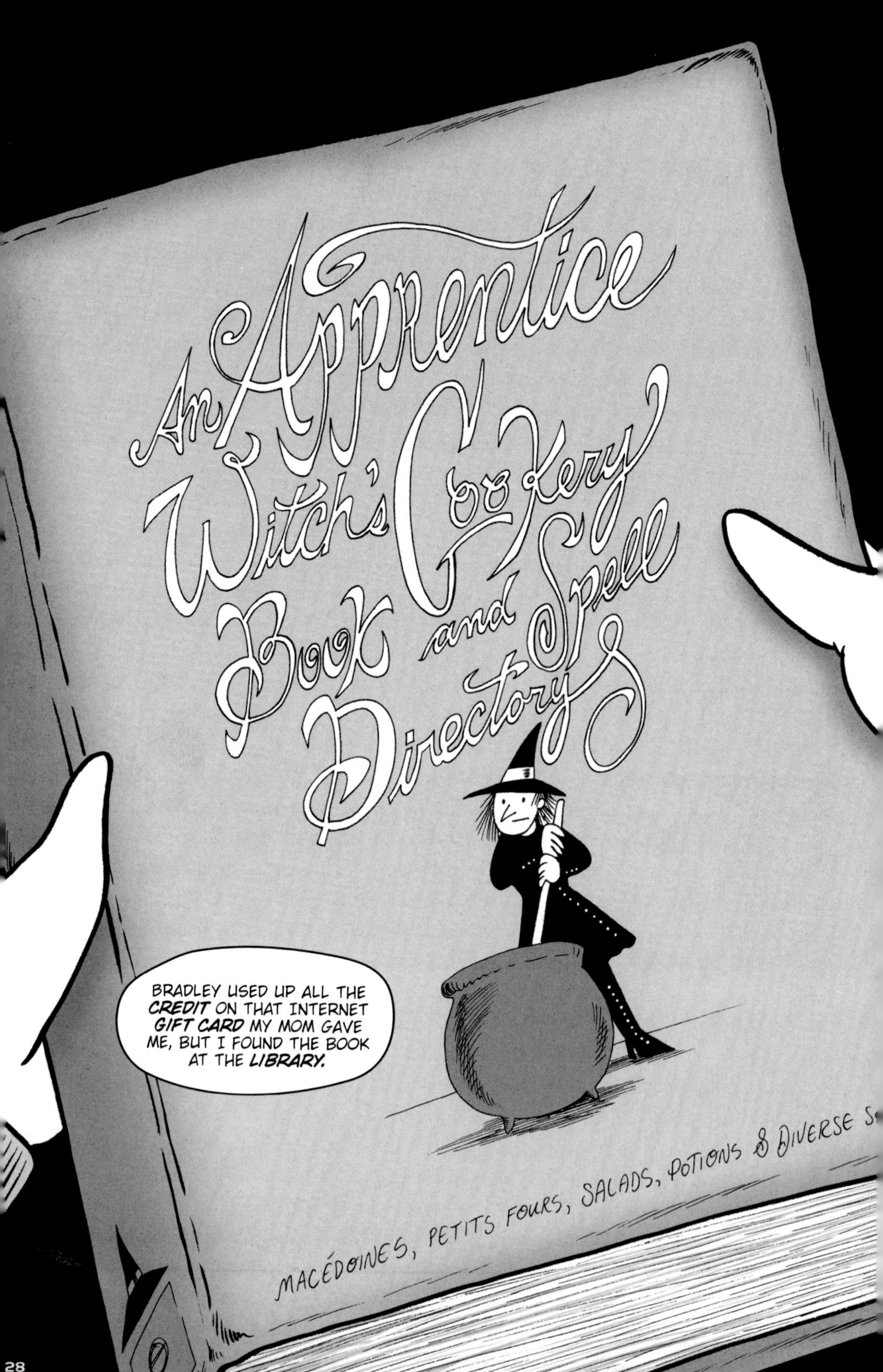
An Apprentice Witch's Cookery Book and Spell Directory
BRADLEY USED UP ALL THE **CREDIT** ON THAT INTERNET **GIFT CARD** MY MOM GAVE ME, BUT I FOUND THE BOOK AT THE **LIBRARY.**
MACÉDOINES, PETITS FOURS, SALADS, POTIONS & DIVERSE

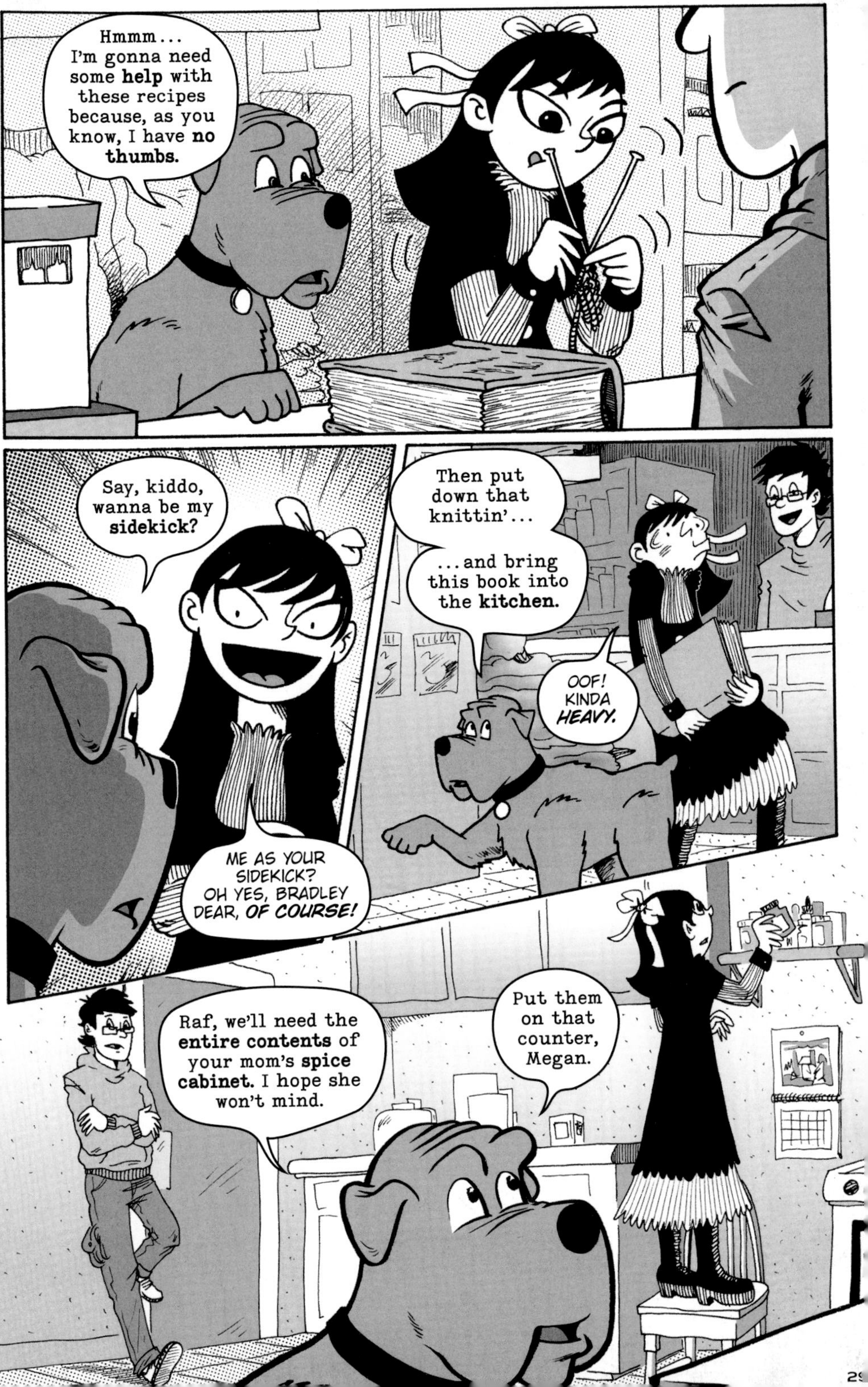
Hmmm... I'm gonna need some help with these recipes because, as you know, I have no thumbs.
Say, kiddo, wanna be my sidekick?
ME AS YOUR SIDEKICK? OH YES, BRADLEY DEAR, OF COURSE!
Then put down that knittin'...
...and bring this book into the kitchen.
OOF! KINDA HEAVY.
Raf, we'll need the entire contents of your mom's spice cabinet. I hope she won't mind.
Put them on that counter, Megan.

CHAPTER FOUR: THE IRONIC CHEF

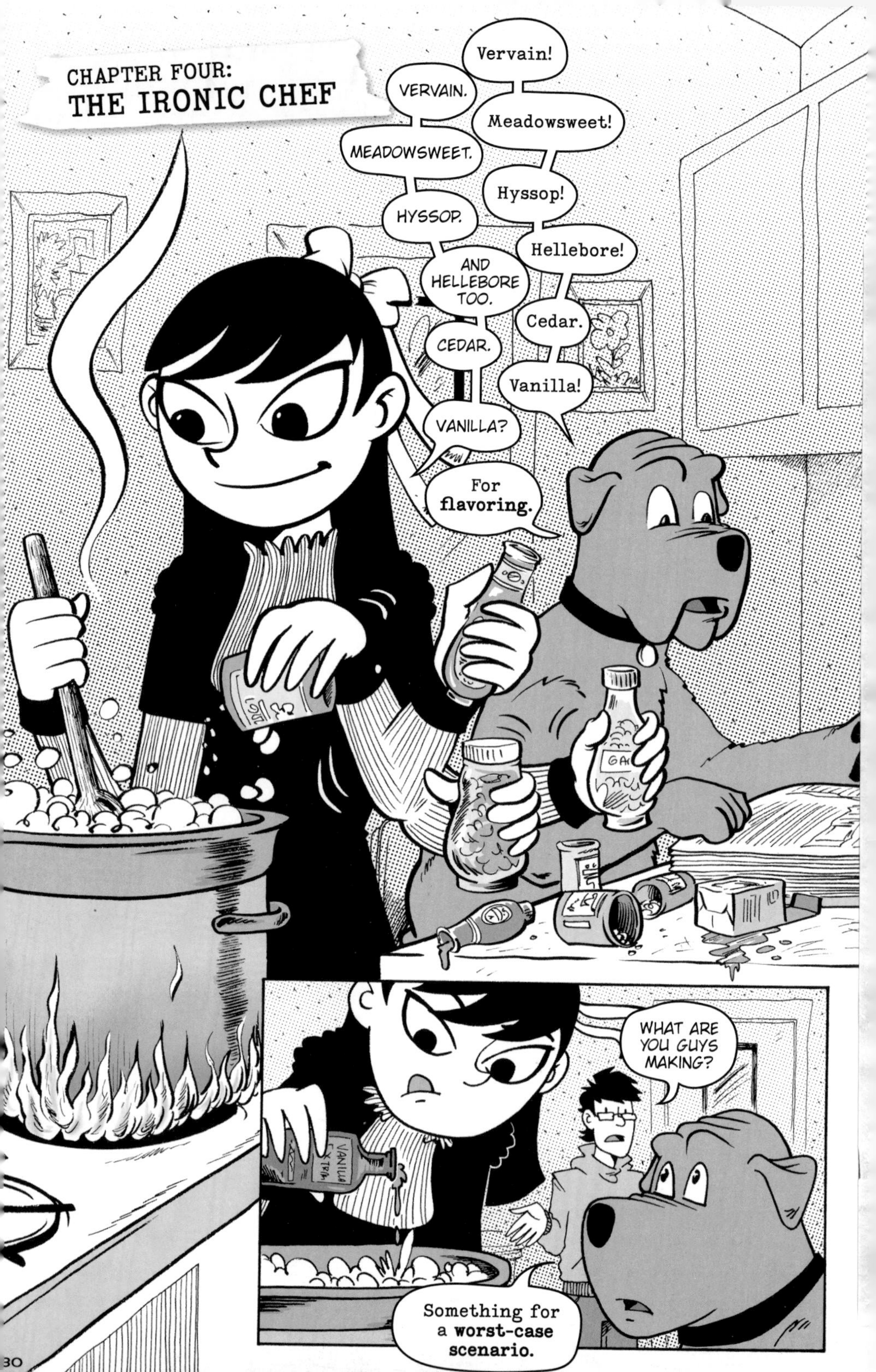
Vervain!
VERVAIN.
Meadowsweet!
MEADOWSWEET.
Hyssop!
HYSSOP.
Hellebore!
AND HELLEBORE TOO.
Cedar.
CEDAR.
Vanilla!
VANILLA?
For **flavoring.**
VANILLA EXTRAC
WHAT ARE YOU GUYS MAKING?
Something for a **worst-case scenario.**

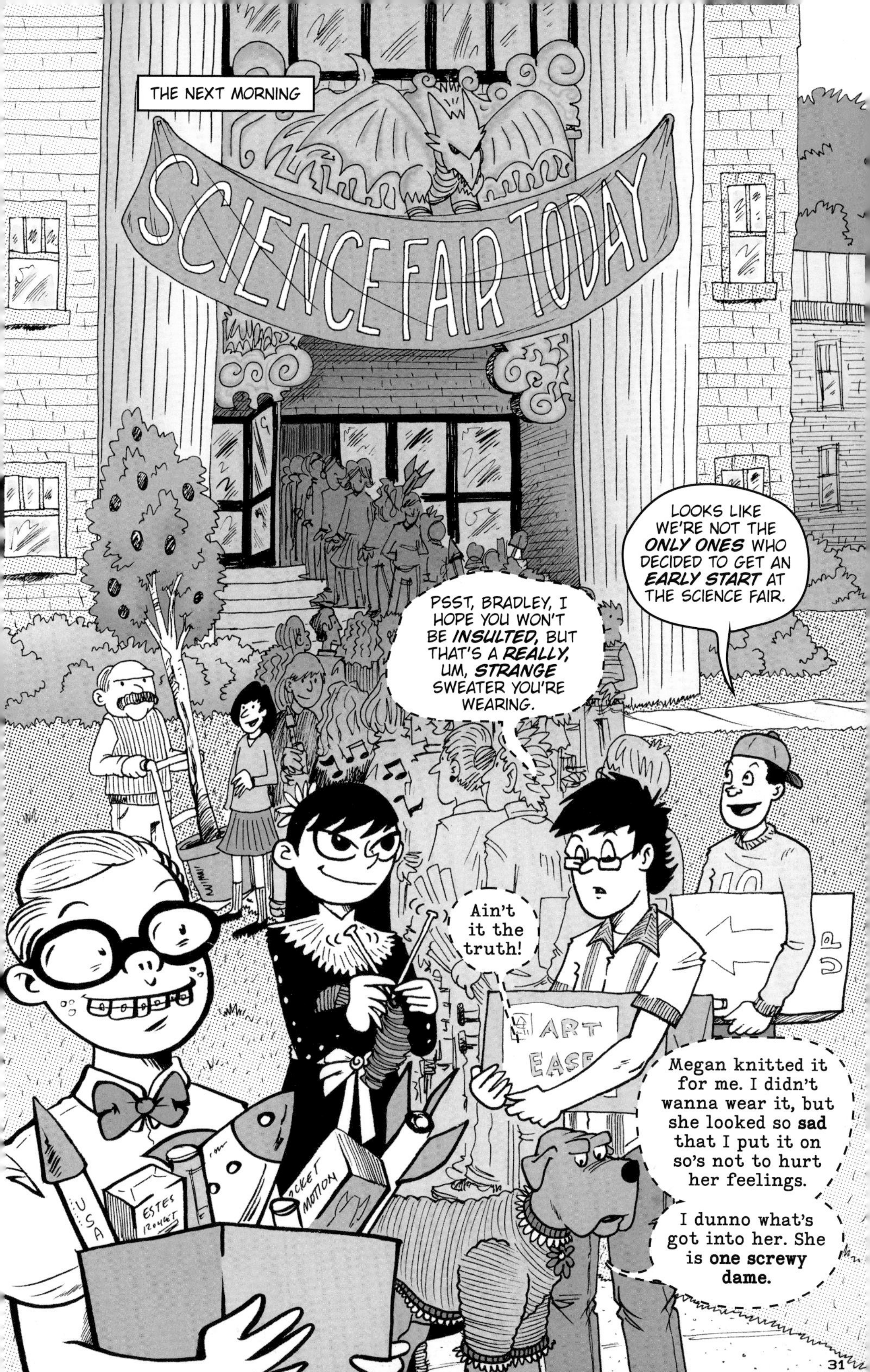
THE NEXT MORNING
SCIENCE FAIR TODAY
LOOKS LIKE WE'RE NOT THE ***ONLY ONES*** WHO DECIDED TO GET AN ***EARLY START*** AT THE SCIENCE FAIR.
PSST, BRADLEY, I HOPE YOU WON'T BE ***INSULTED,*** BUT THAT'S A ***REALLY,*** UM, ***STRANGE*** SWEATER YOU'RE WEARING.
Ain't it the truth!
Megan knitted it for me. I didn't wanna wear it, but she looked so **sad** that I put it on so's not to hurt her feelings.
I dunno what's got into her. She is **one screwy dame.**
ART EASE
ESTES ROCKET
ROCKET MOTION
USA

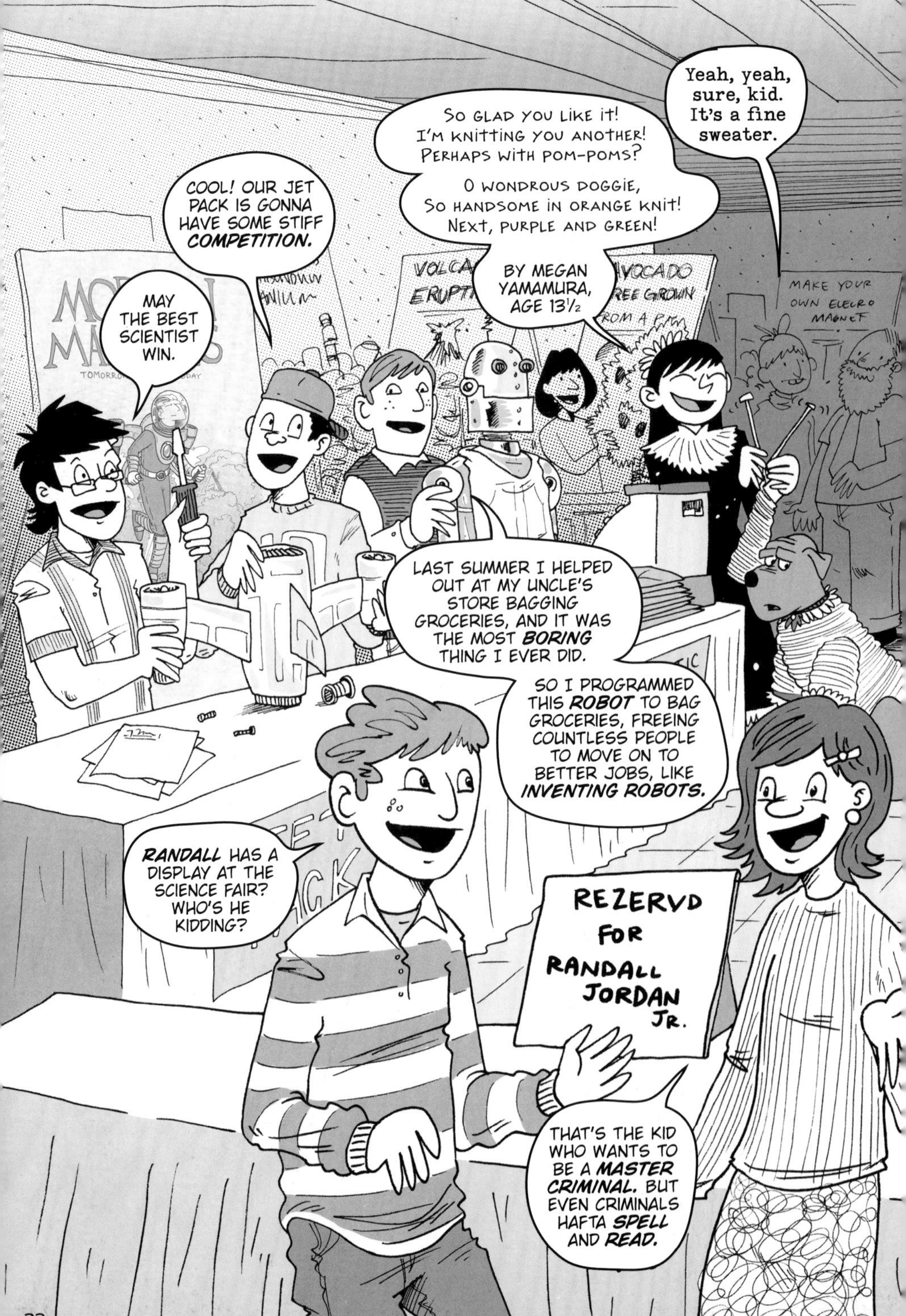
MAY THE BEST SCIENTIST WIN.
COOL! OUR JET PACK IS GONNA HAVE SOME STIFF COMPETITION.
SO GLAD YOU LIKE IT! I'M KNITTING YOU ANOTHER! PERHAPS WITH POM-POMS?
O WONDROUS DOGGIE, SO HANDSOME IN ORANGE KNIT! NEXT, PURPLE AND GREEN!
BY MEGAN YAMAMURA, AGE 13½
Yeah, yeah, sure, kid. It's a fine sweater.
MAKE YOUR OWN ELECRO MAGNET
LAST SUMMER I HELPED OUT AT MY UNCLE'S STORE BAGGING GROCERIES, AND IT WAS THE MOST BORING THING I EVER DID.
SO I PROGRAMMED THIS ROBOT TO BAG GROCERIES, FREEING COUNTLESS PEOPLE TO MOVE ON TO BETTER JOBS, LIKE INVENTING ROBOTS.
RANDALL HAS A DISPLAY AT THE SCIENCE FAIR? WHO'S HE KIDDING?
REZERVD FOR RANDALL JORDAN JR.
THAT'S THE KID WHO WANTS TO BE A MASTER CRIMINAL. BUT EVEN CRIMINALS HAFTA SPELL AND READ.

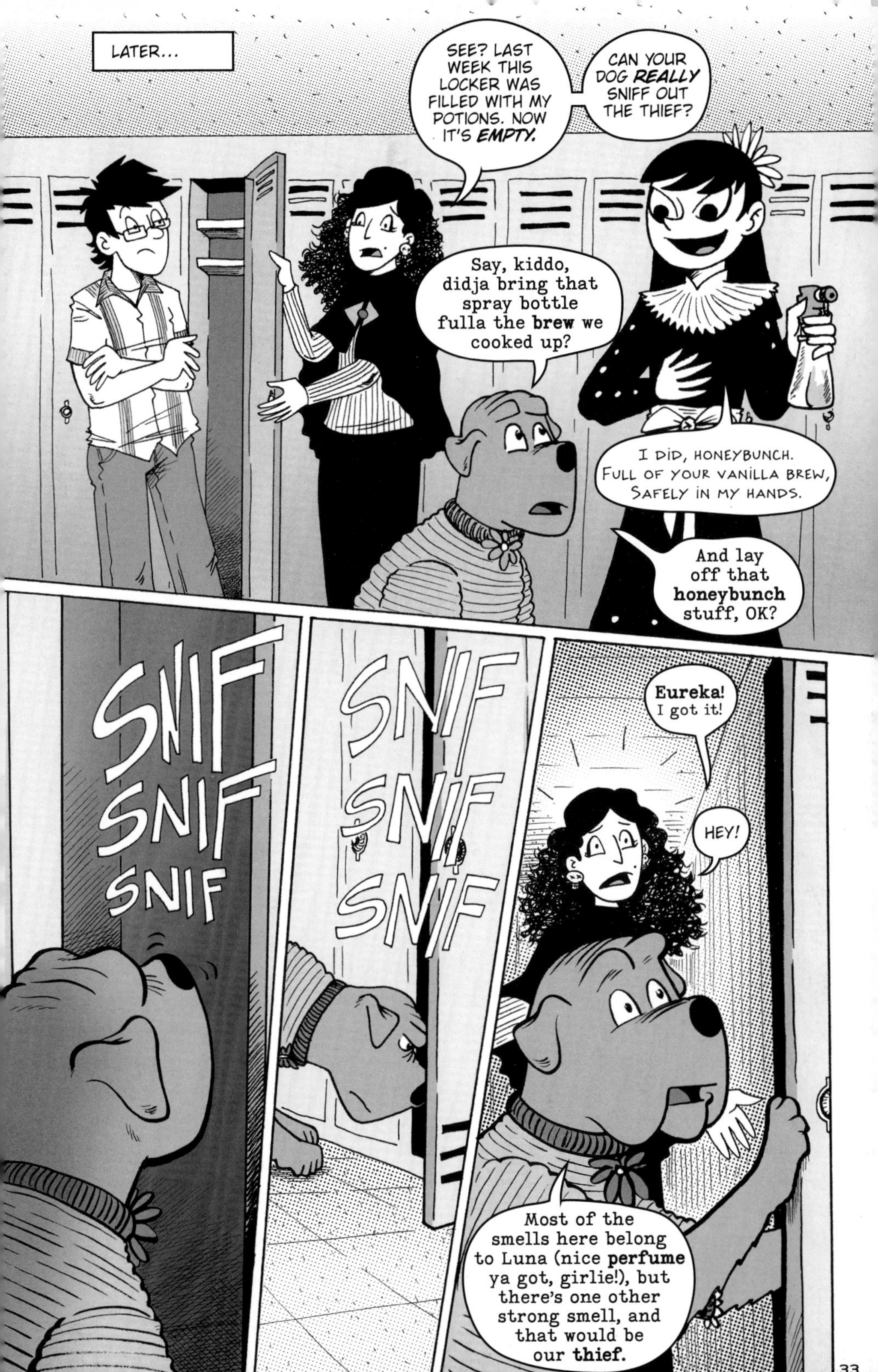
LATER...
SEE? LAST WEEK THIS LOCKER WAS FILLED WITH MY POTIONS. NOW IT'S EMPTY.
CAN YOUR DOG REALLY SNIFF OUT THE THIEF?
Say, kiddo, didja bring that spray bottle fulla the brew we cooked up?
I DID, HONEYBUNCH. FULL OF YOUR VANILLA BREW, SAFELY IN MY HANDS.
And lay off that honeybunch stuff, OK?
SNIF SNIF SNIF
SNIF SNIF SNIF
Eureka! I got it!
HEY!
Most of the smells here belong to Luna (nice perfume ya got, girlie!), but there's one other strong smell, and that would be our thief.

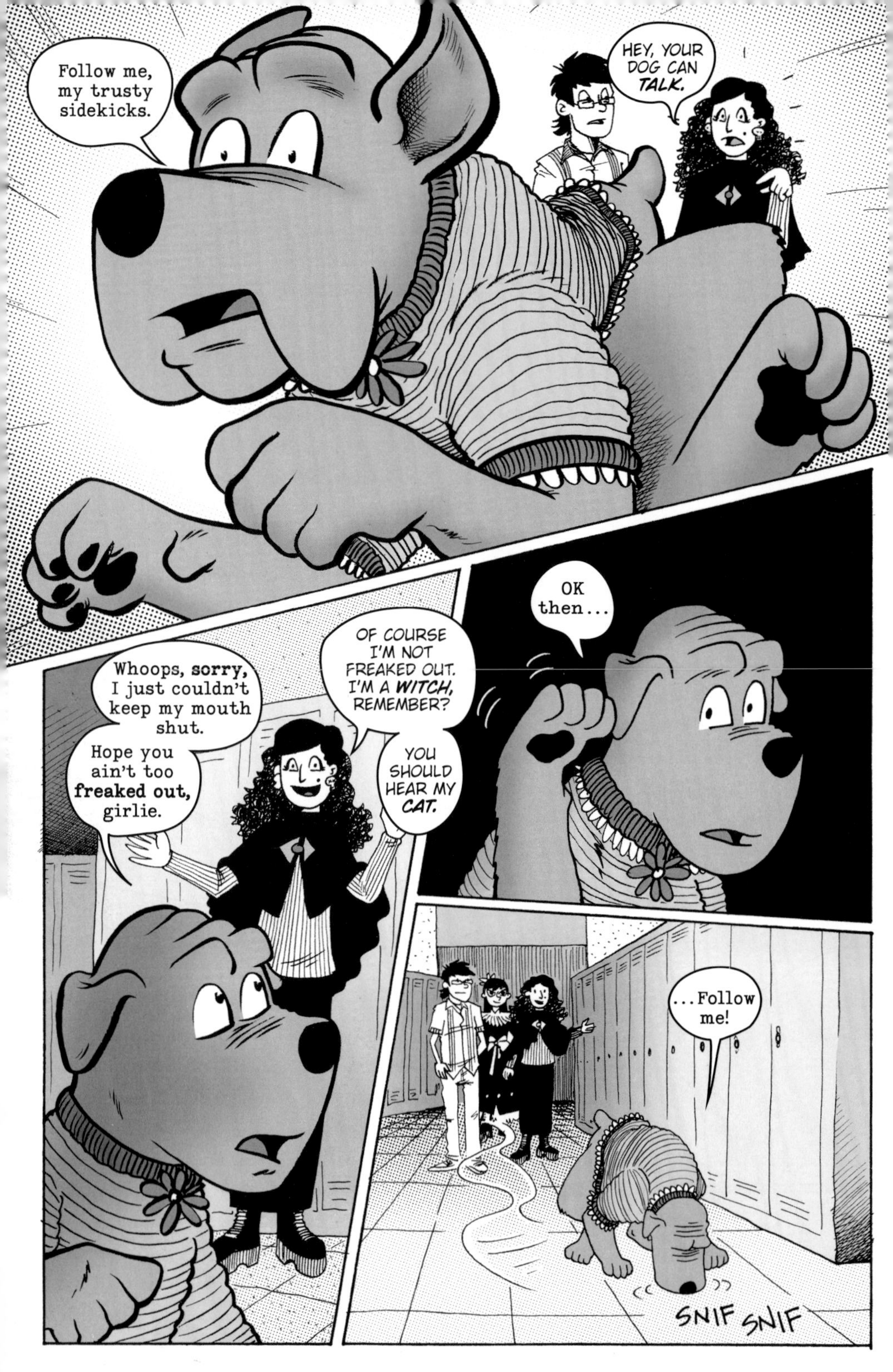
Follow me, my trusty sidekicks.
HEY, YOUR DOG CAN TALK.
OK then...
Whoops, sorry, I just couldn't keep my mouth shut.
Hope you ain't too freaked out, girlie.
OF COURSE I'M NOT FREAKED OUT. I'M A WITCH, REMEMBER?
YOU SHOULD HEAR MY CAT.
...Follow me!
SNIF SNIF

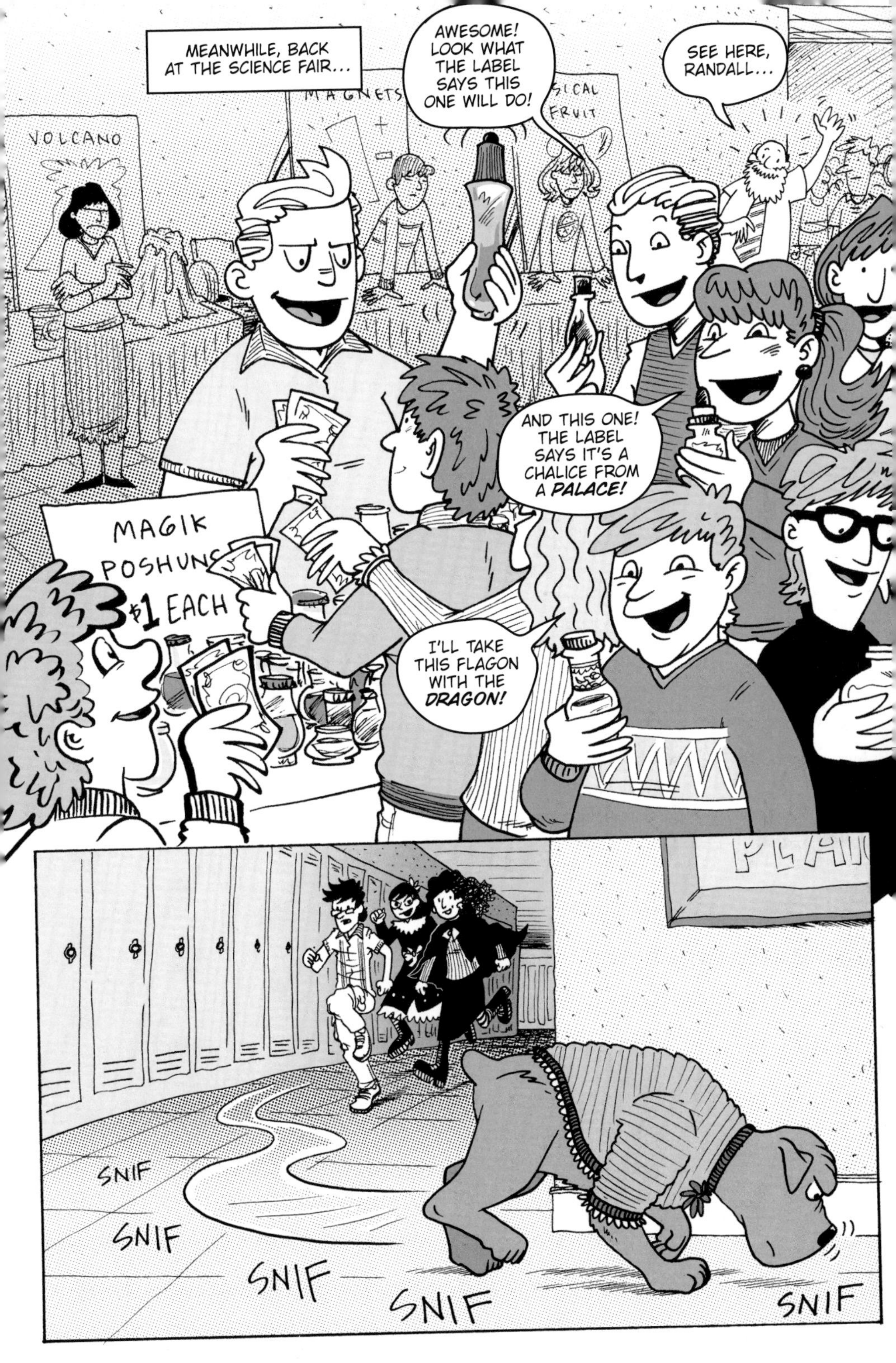
MEANWHILE, BACK AT THE SCIENCE FAIR...
AWESOME! LOOK WHAT THE LABEL SAYS THIS ONE WILL DO!
SEE HERE, RANDALL...
VOLCANO
MAGNETS
AND THIS ONE! THE LABEL SAYS IT'S A CHALICE FROM A PALACE!
MAGIK POSHUNS $1 EACH
I'LL TAKE THIS FLAGON WITH THE DRAGON!
SNIF
SNIF
SNIF
SNIF
SNIF

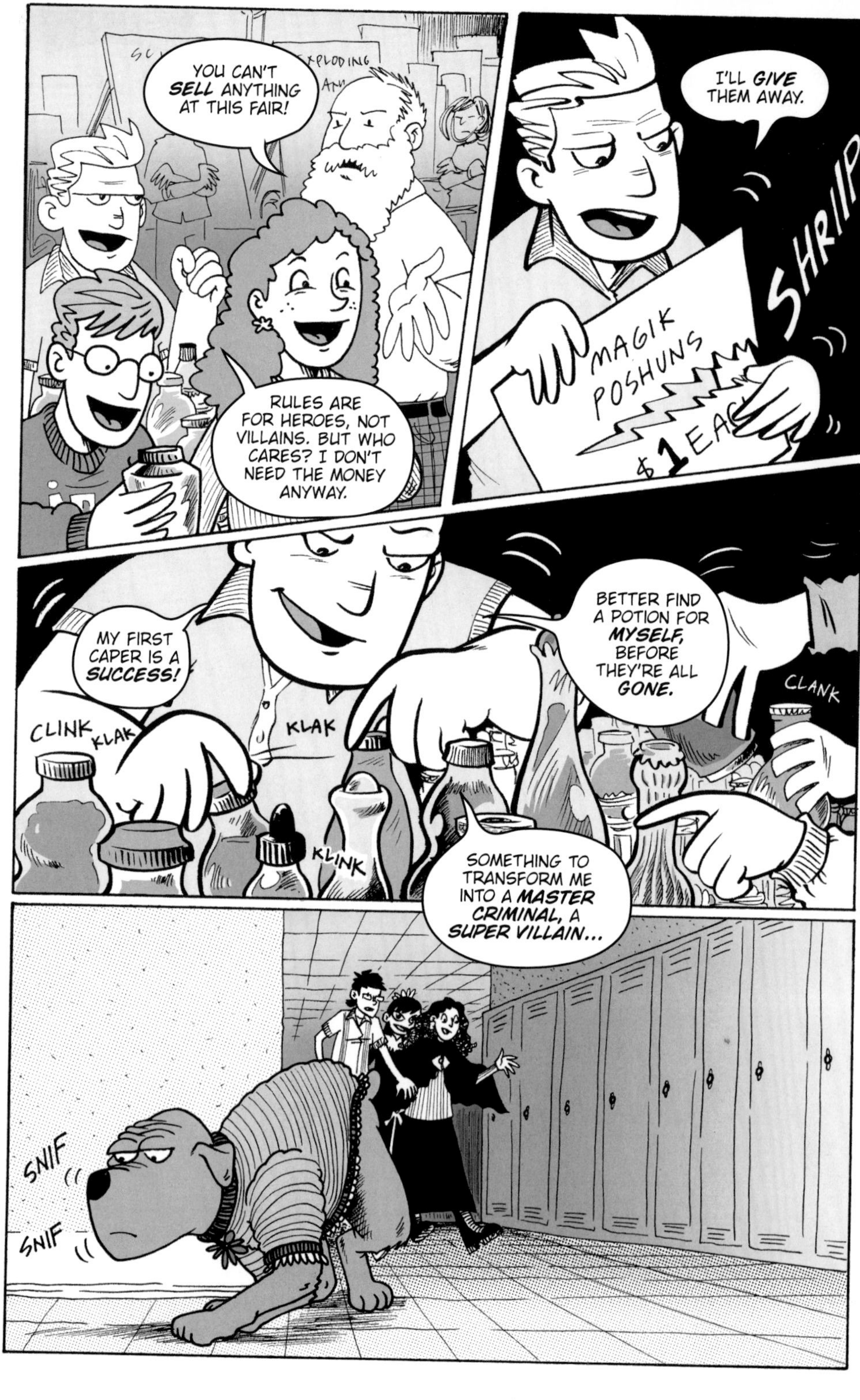

EXPLODING
YOU CAN'T SELL ANYTHING AT THIS FAIR!
RULES ARE FOR HEROES, NOT VILLAINS. BUT WHO CARES? I DON'T NEED THE MONEY ANYWAY.
I'LL GIVE THEM AWAY.
MAGIK POSHUNS $1 EAC
SHRIIP
MY FIRST CAPER IS A SUCCESS!
BETTER FIND A POTION FOR MYSELF, BEFORE THEY'RE ALL GONE.
CLANK
CLINK
KLAK
KLAK
KLINK
SOMETHING TO TRANSFORM ME INTO A MASTER CRIMINAL, A SUPER VILLAIN...
SNIF
SNIF

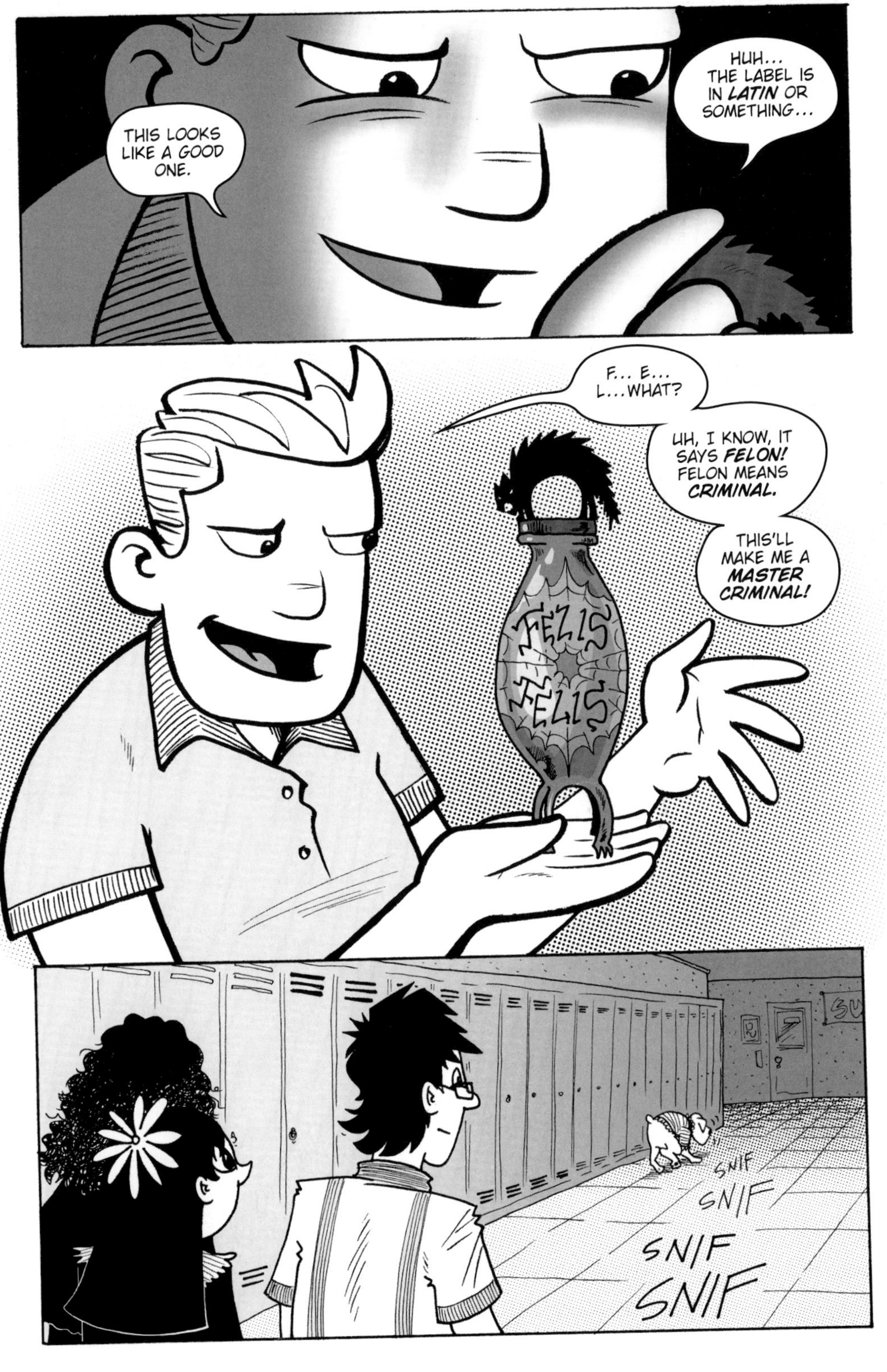
THIS LOOKS LIKE A GOOD ONE.
HUH... THE LABEL IS IN LATIN OR SOMETHING...
F... E... L...WHAT?
UH, I KNOW, IT SAYS FELON! FELON MEANS CRIMINAL.
THIS'LL MAKE ME A MASTER CRIMINAL!
FELIS FELIS
SNIF
SNIF
SNIF
SNIF

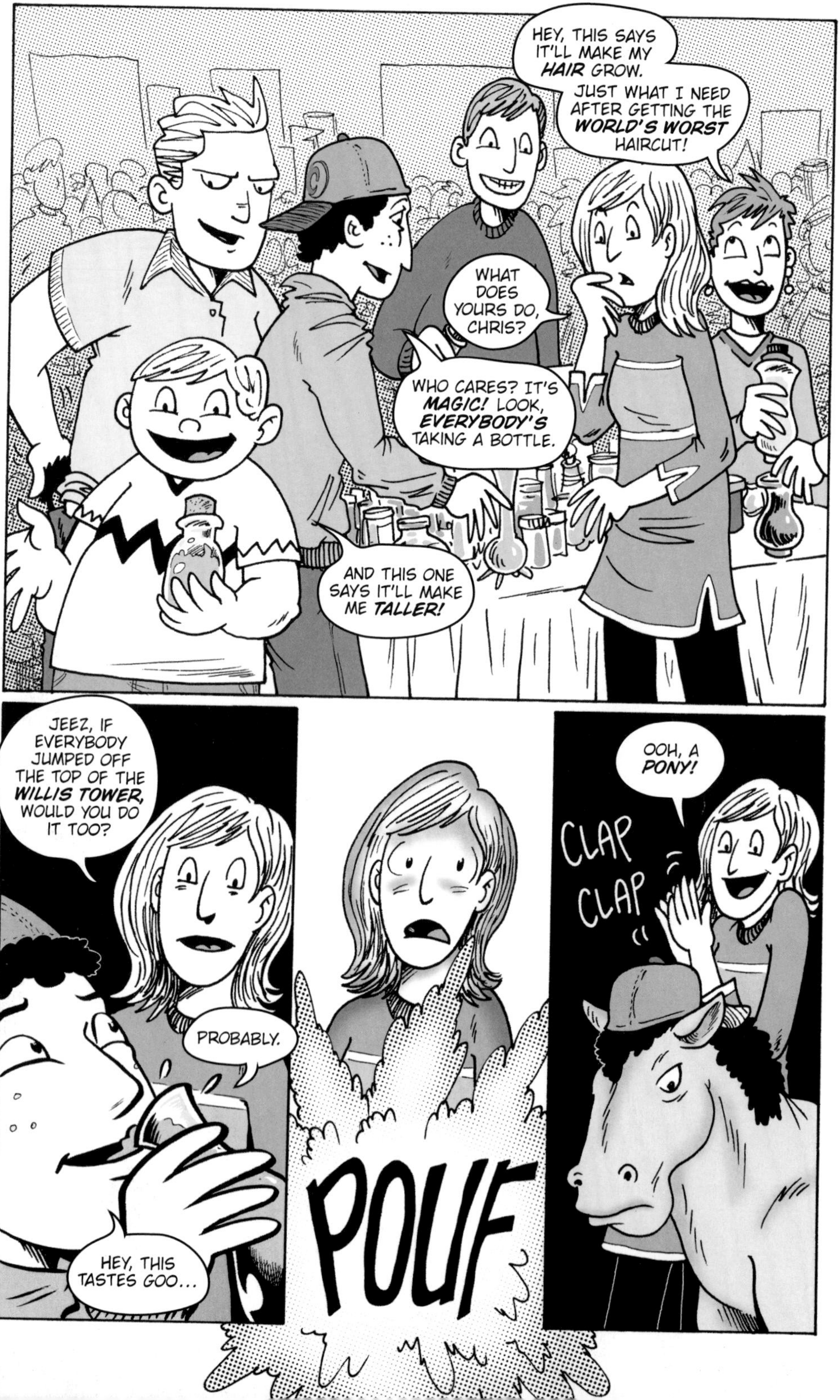
HEY, THIS SAYS IT'LL MAKE MY HAIR GROW.
JUST WHAT I NEED AFTER GETTING THE WORLD'S WORST HAIRCUT!
WHAT DOES YOURS DO, CHRIS?
WHO CARES? IT'S MAGIC! LOOK, EVERYBODY'S TAKING A BOTTLE.
AND THIS ONE SAYS IT'LL MAKE ME TALLER!
JEEZ, IF EVERYBODY JUMPED OFF THE TOP OF THE WILLIS TOWER, WOULD YOU DO IT TOO?
PROBABLY.
HEY, THIS TASTES GOO...
POUF
OOH, A PONY!
CLAP
CLAP

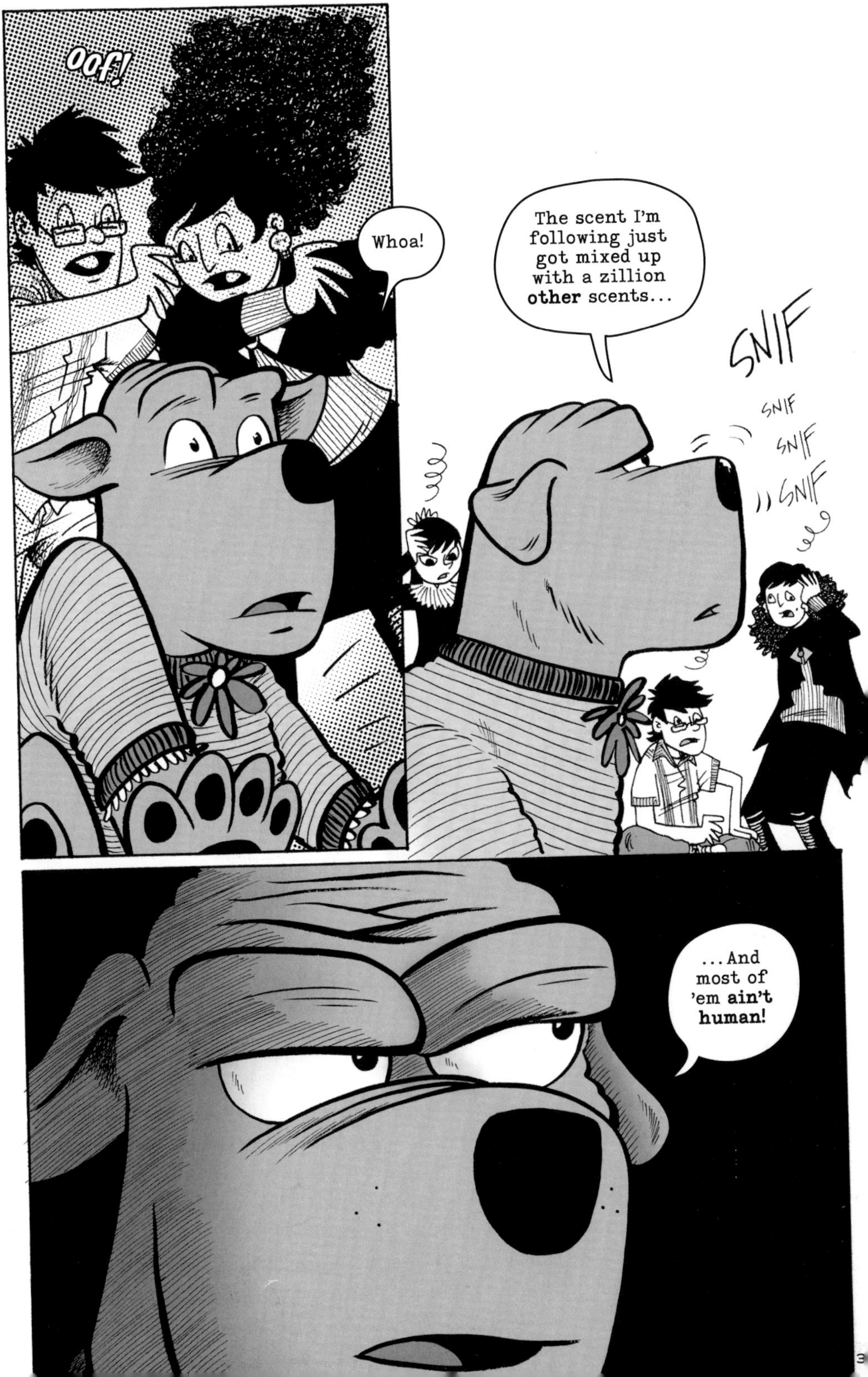
OOF!
Whoa!
The scent I'm following just got mixed up with a zillion **other** scents...
SNIF
SNIF
SNIF
SNIF
...And most of 'em **ain't human!**

CHAPTER FIVE: NOT FAIR!

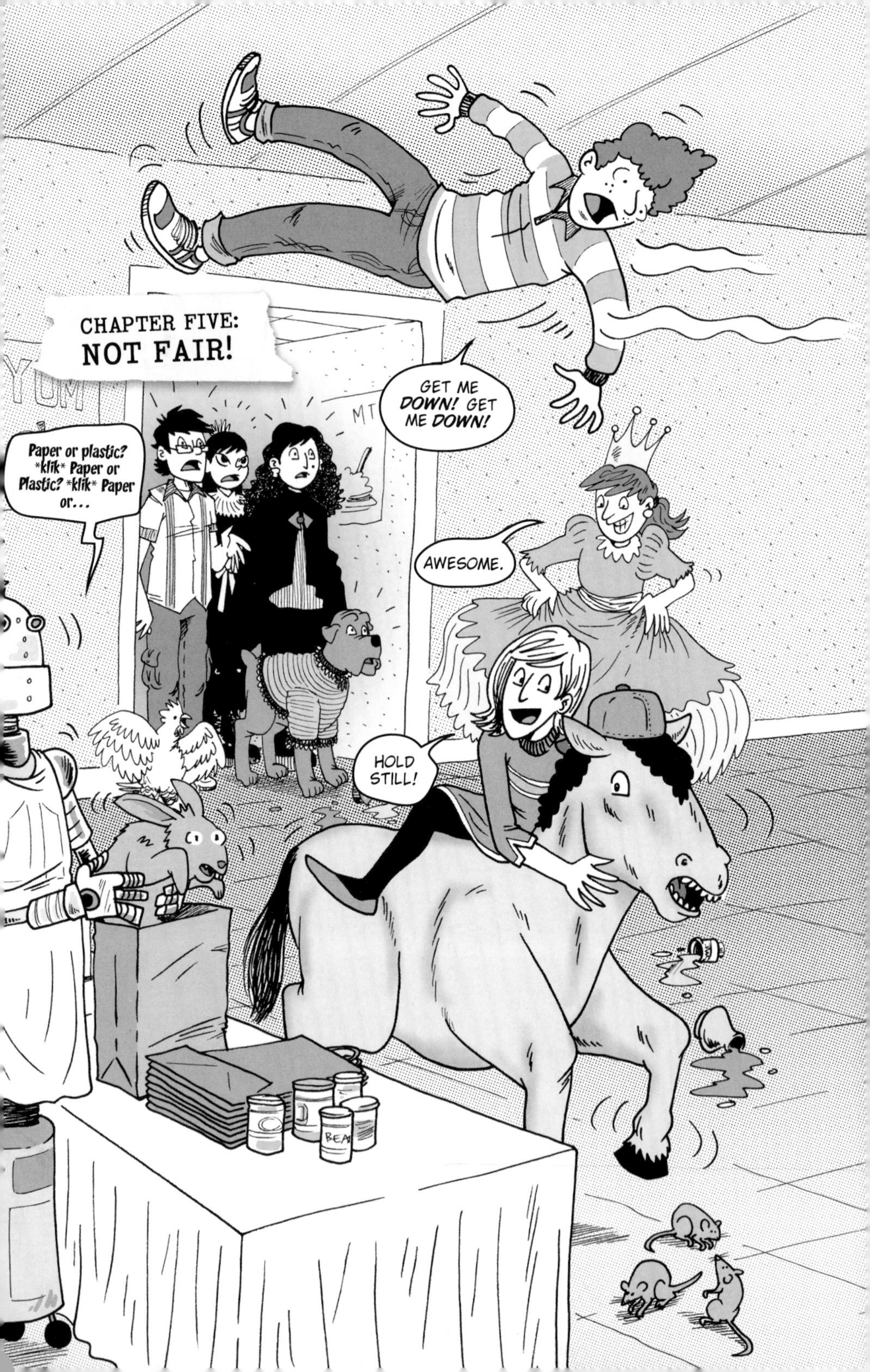
GET ME DOWN! GET ME DOWN!
Paper or plastic? *klik* Paper or Plastic? *klik* Paper or...
AWESOME.
HOLD STILL!

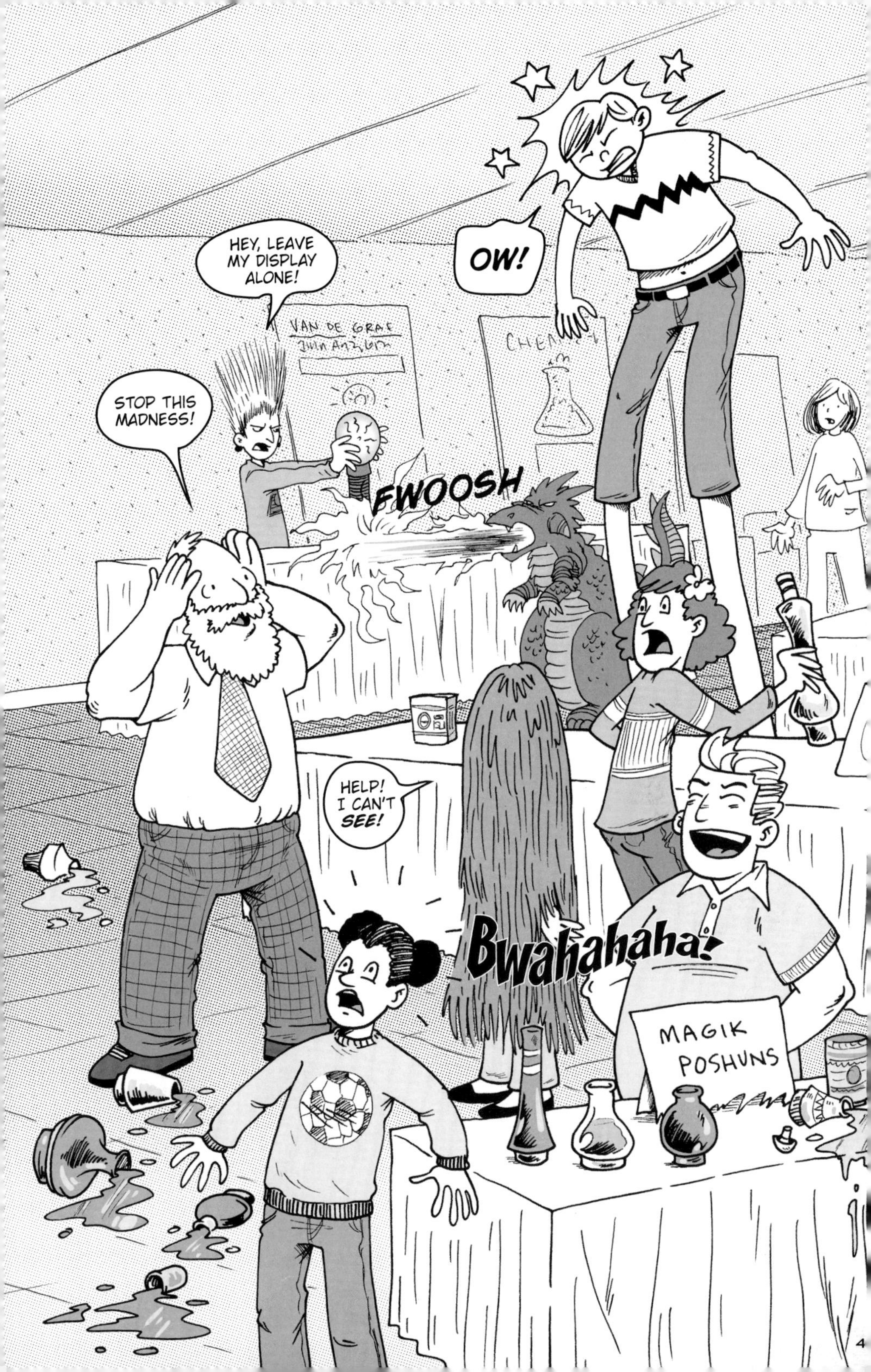
HEY, LEAVE MY DISPLAY ALONE!
OW!
VAN DE GRAF
STOP THIS MADNESS!
FWOOSH
HELP! I CAN'T SEE!
Bwahahaha!
MAGIK POSHUNS

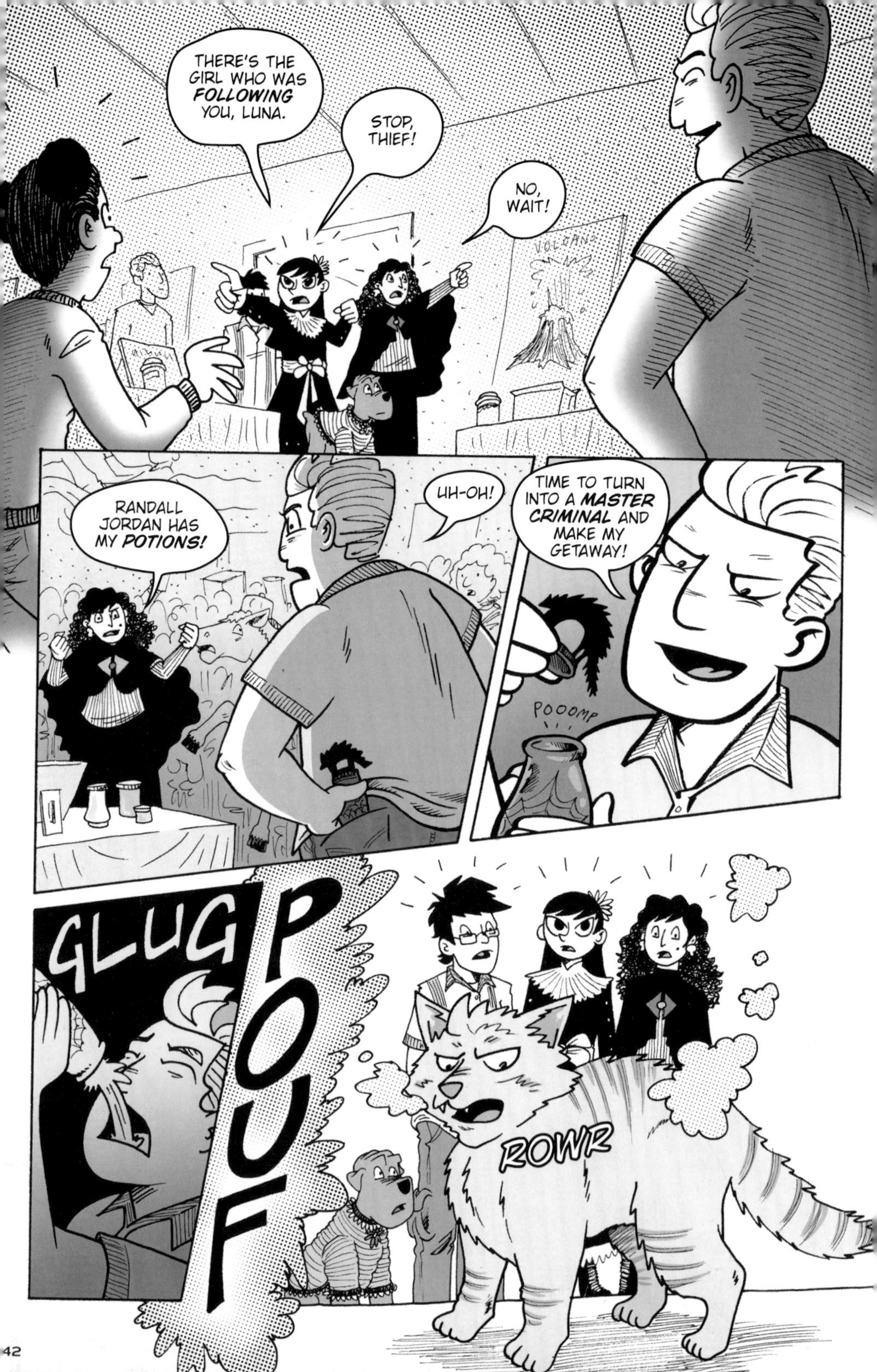
THERE'S THE GIRL WHO WAS *FOLLOWING* YOU, LUNA.
STOP, THIEF!
NO, WAIT!
VOLCANO
RANDALL JORDAN HAS MY *POTIONS!*
UH-OH!
TIME TO TURN INTO A *MASTER CRIMINAL* AND MAKE MY GETAWAY!
POOOMP
GLUG
POUF
ROWR

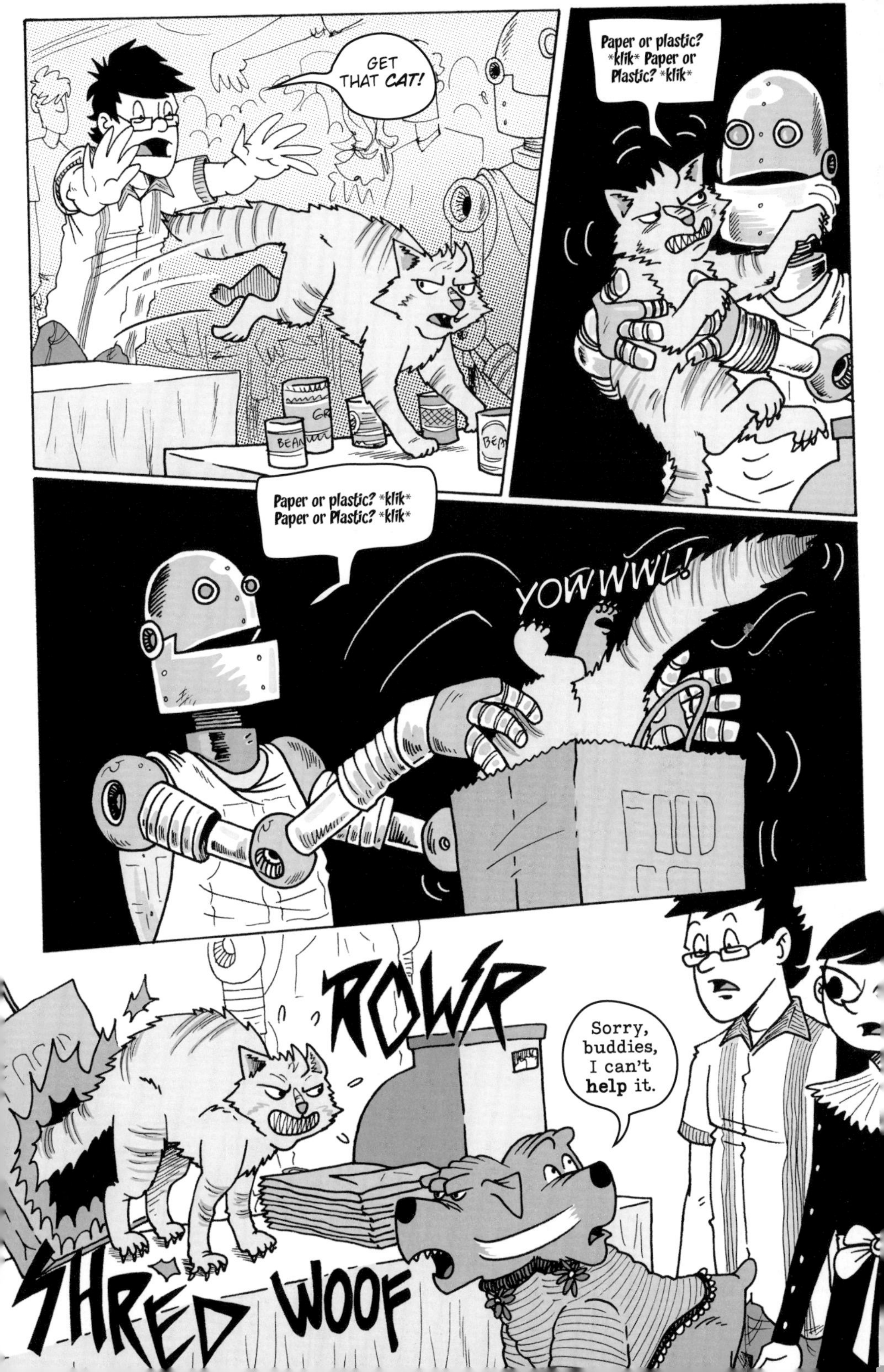
GET THAT CAT!
BEAN
BEA
Paper or plastic? *klik* Paper or Plastic? *klik*
Paper or plastic? *klik* Paper or Plastic? *klik*
YOWWWL!
FOOD
ROWR
Sorry, buddies, I can't help it.
SHRED
WOOF

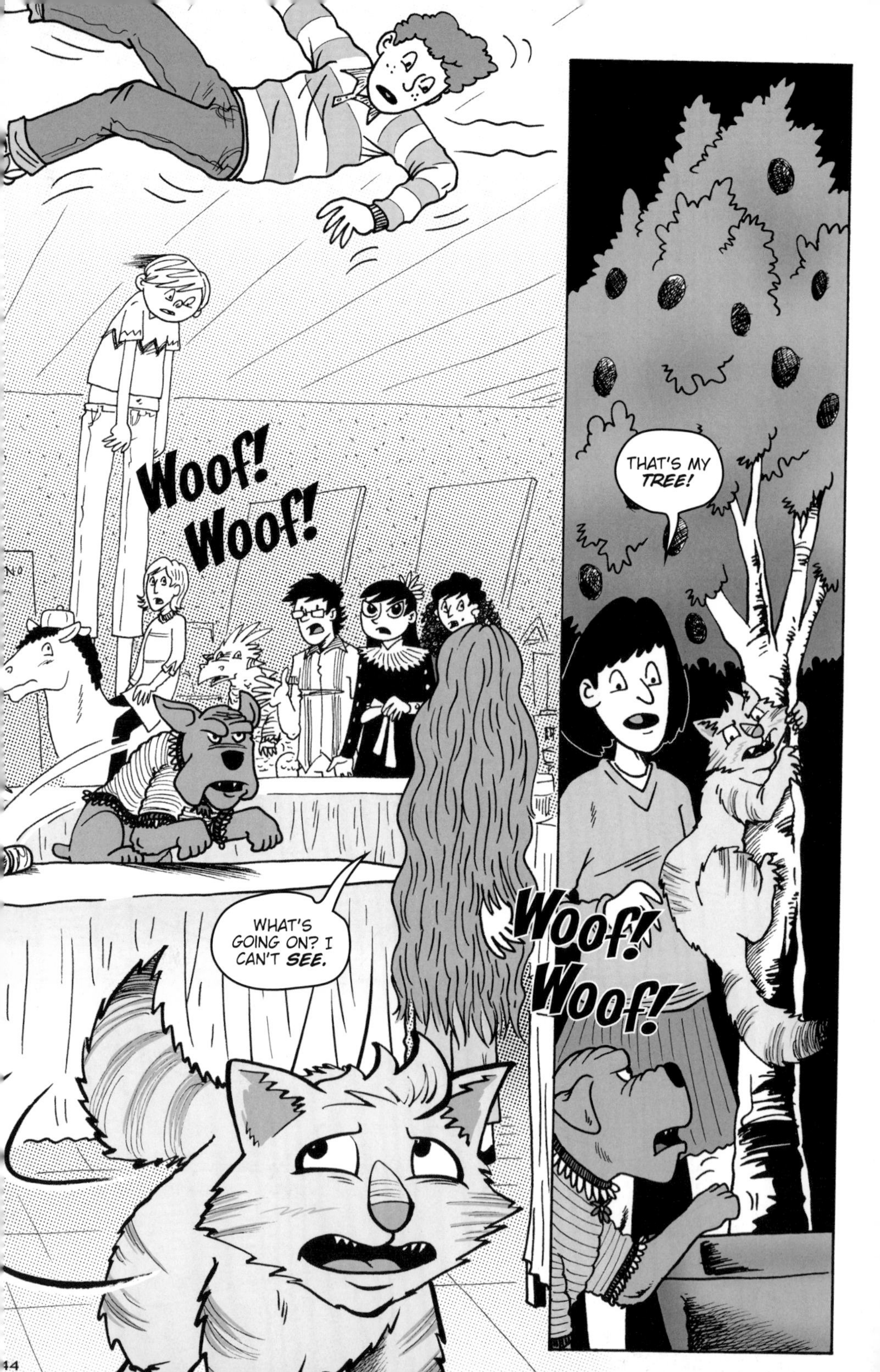
Woof! Woof!
THAT'S MY TREE!
WHAT'S GOING ON? I CAN'T SEE.
Woof! Woof!

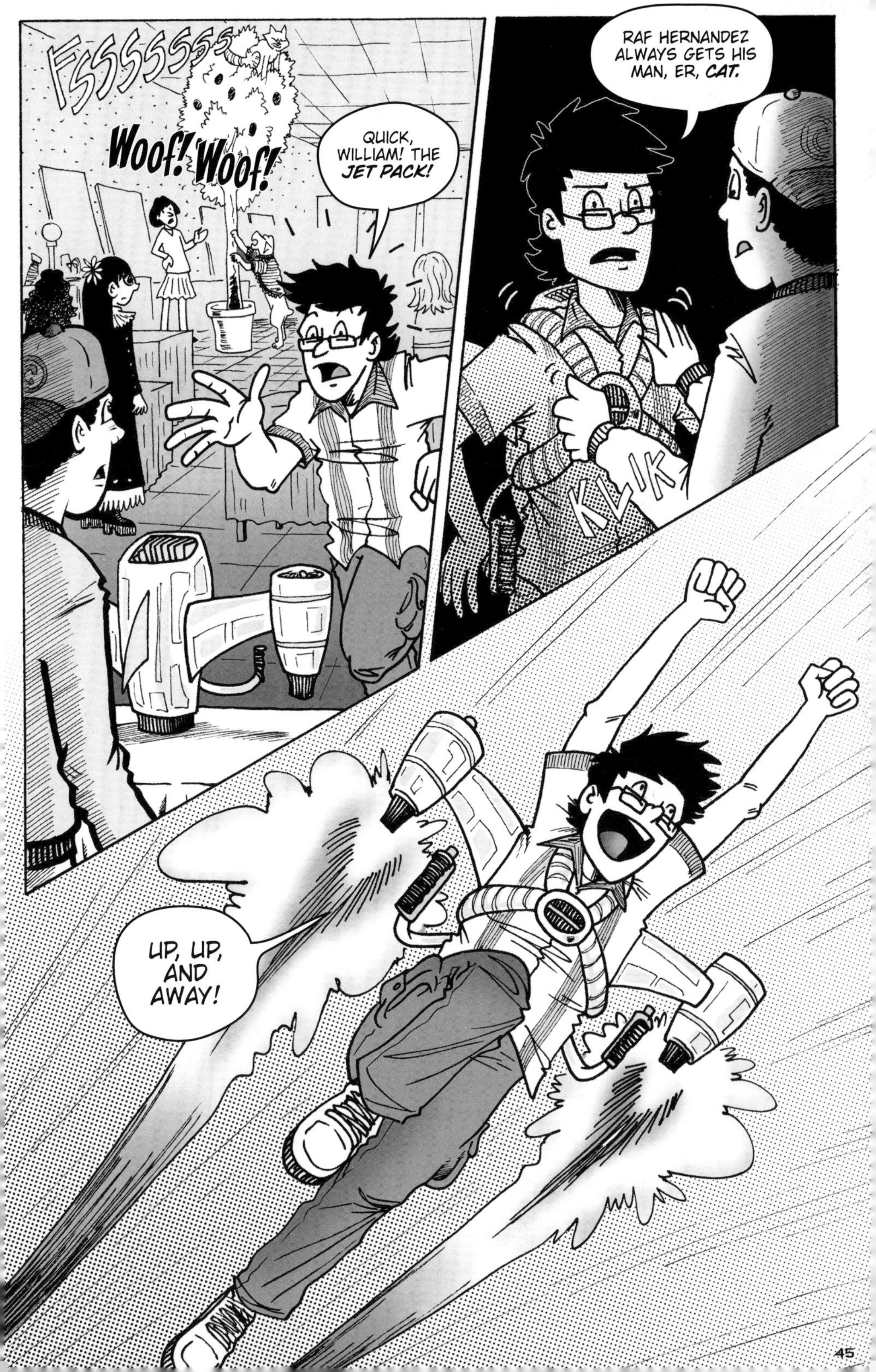
FSSSSSSSS
WOOF! WOOF!
QUICK, WILLIAM! THE JET PACK!
RAF HERNANDEZ ALWAYS GETS HIS MAN, ER, CAT.
KLIK
UP, UP, AND AWAY!

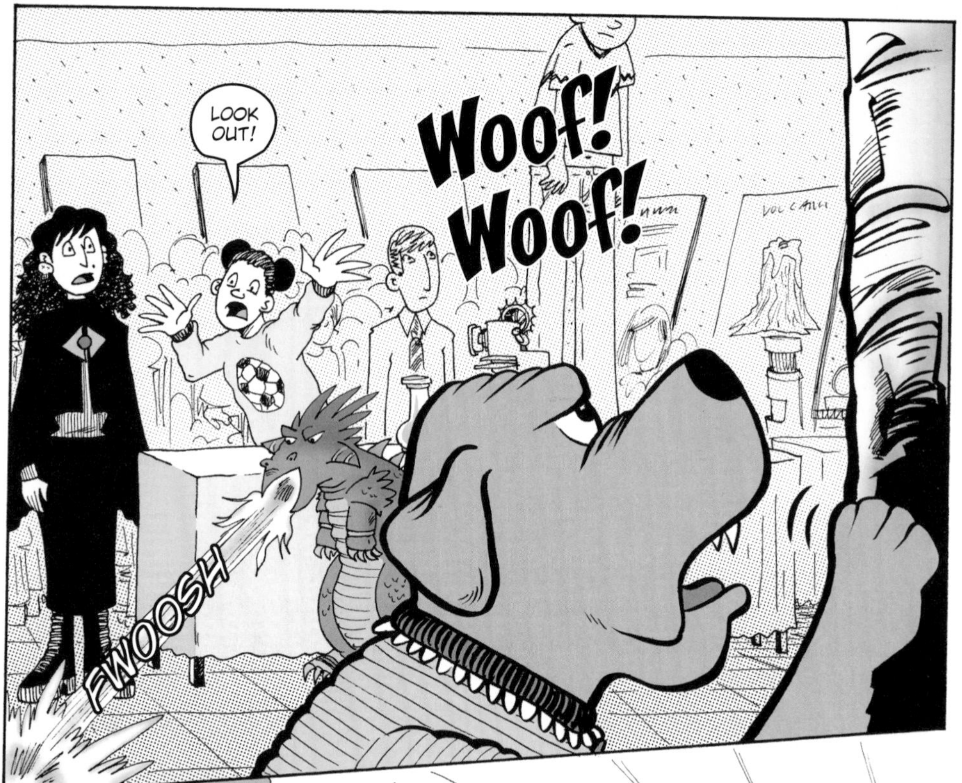
LOOK OUT!
Woof! Woof!
FWOOSH

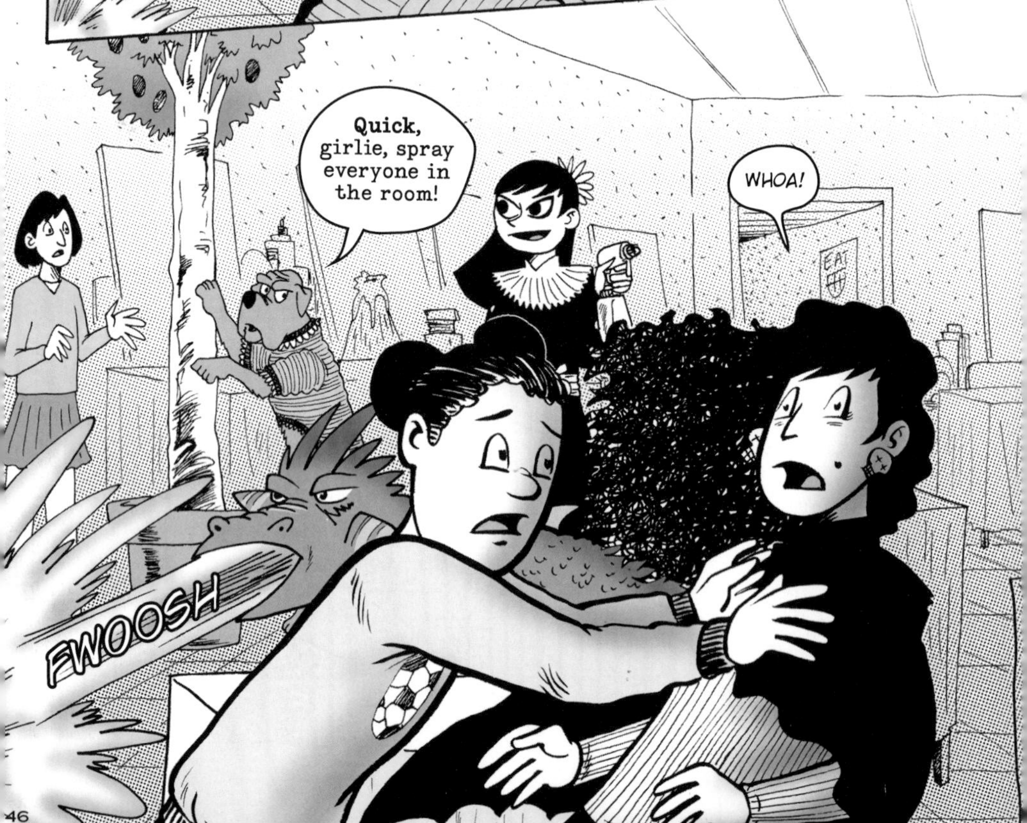
Quick, girlie, spray everyone in the room!
WHOA!
FWOOSH

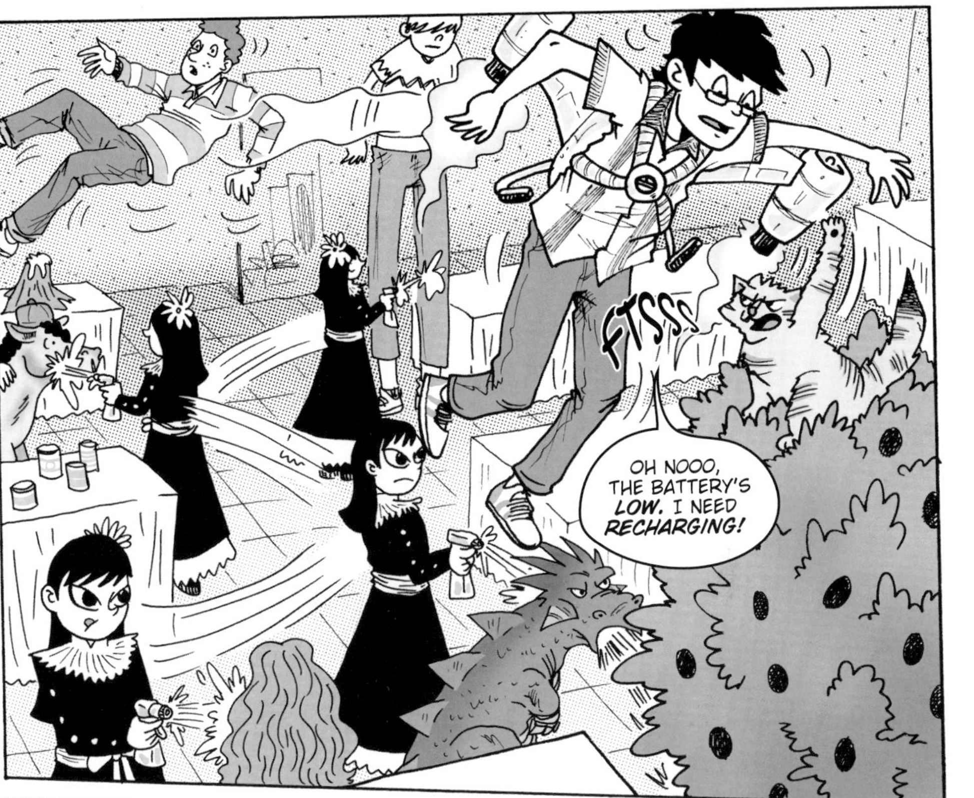
FTSSS
OH NOOO, THE BATTERY'S **LOW.** I NEED **RECHARGING!**

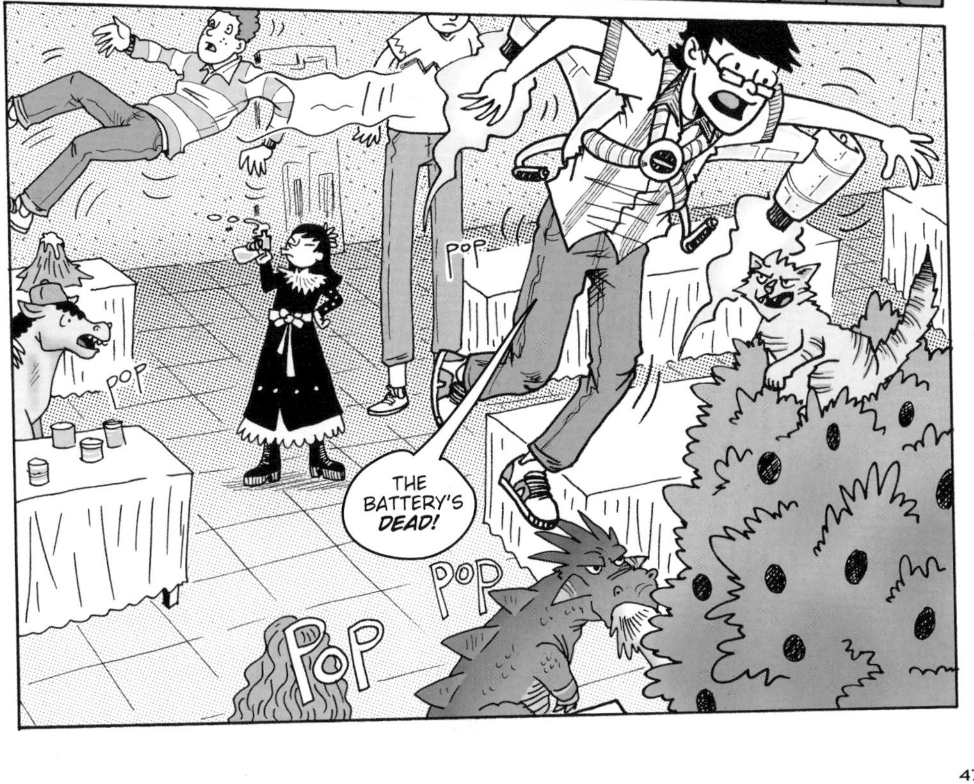
POP
POP
THE BATTERY'S **DEAD!**
POP
POP

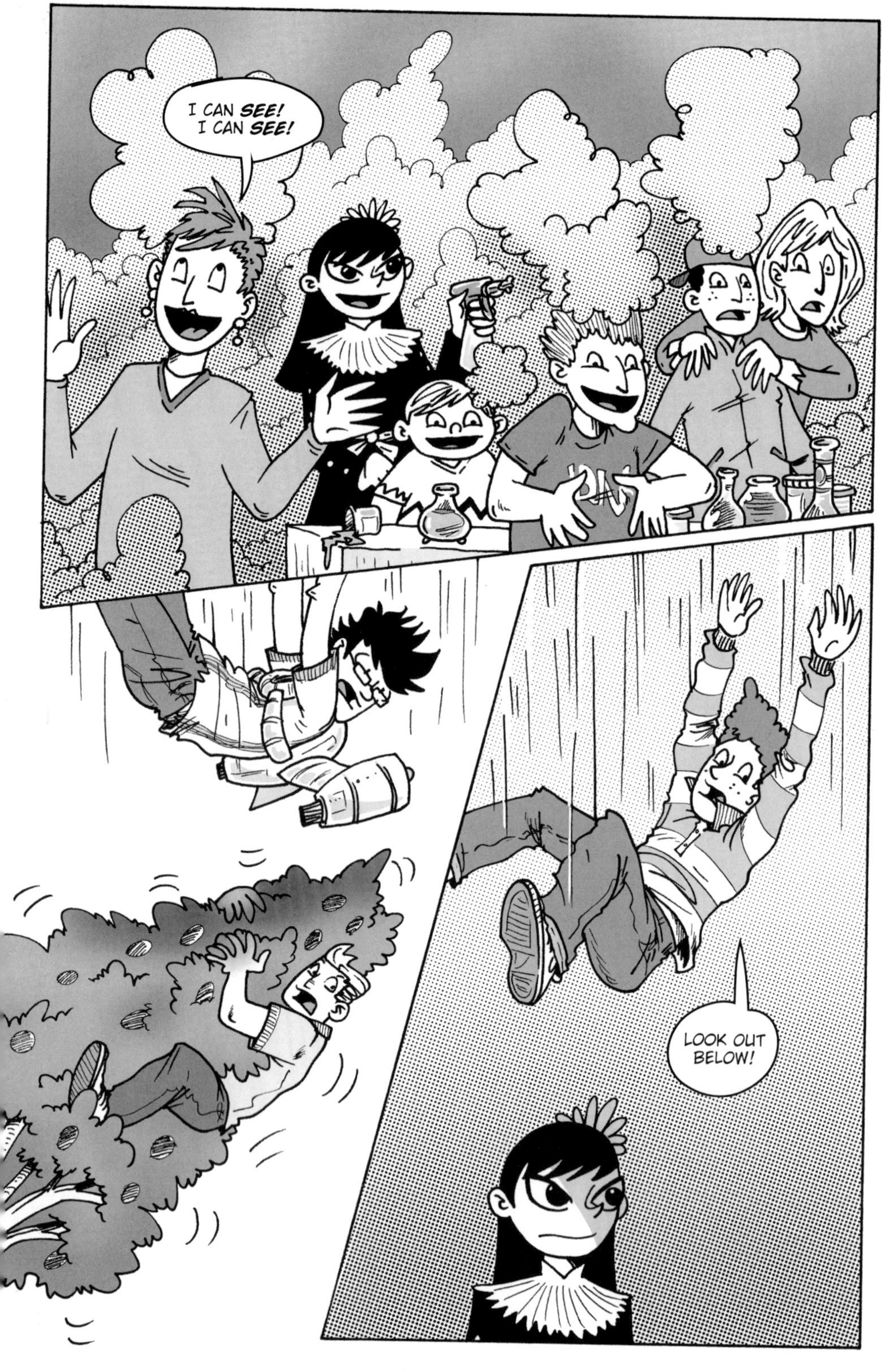
I CAN SEE! I CAN SEE!
LOOK OUT BELOW!

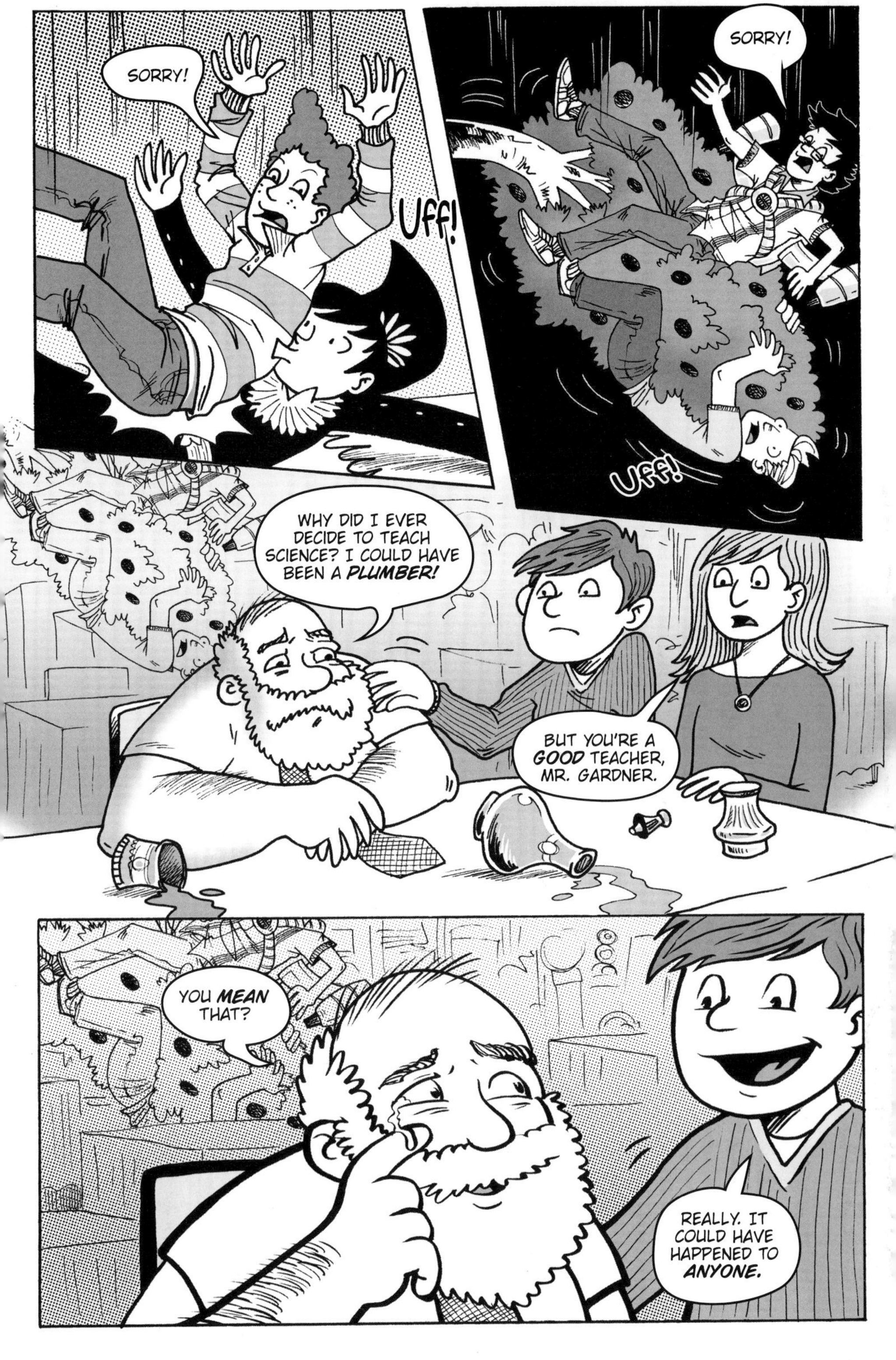
SORRY!
UFF!
SORRY!
UFF!
WHY DID I EVER DECIDE TO TEACH SCIENCE? I COULD HAVE BEEN A PLUMBER!
BUT YOU'RE A GOOD TEACHER, MR. GARDNER.
YOU MEAN THAT?
REALLY. IT COULD HAVE HAPPENED TO ANYONE.

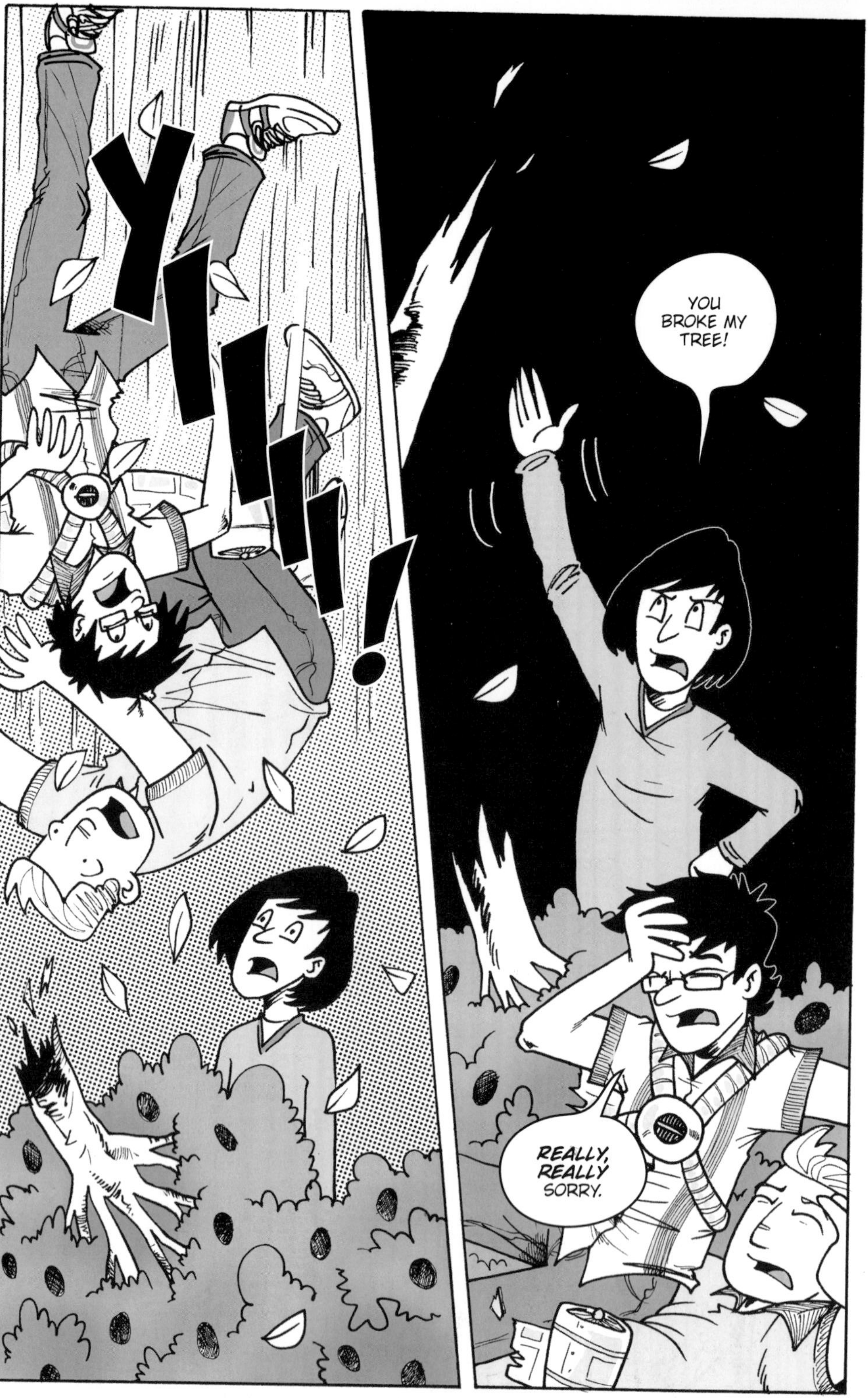
YIIII!
YOU BROKE MY TREE!
REALLY, REALLY SORRY.

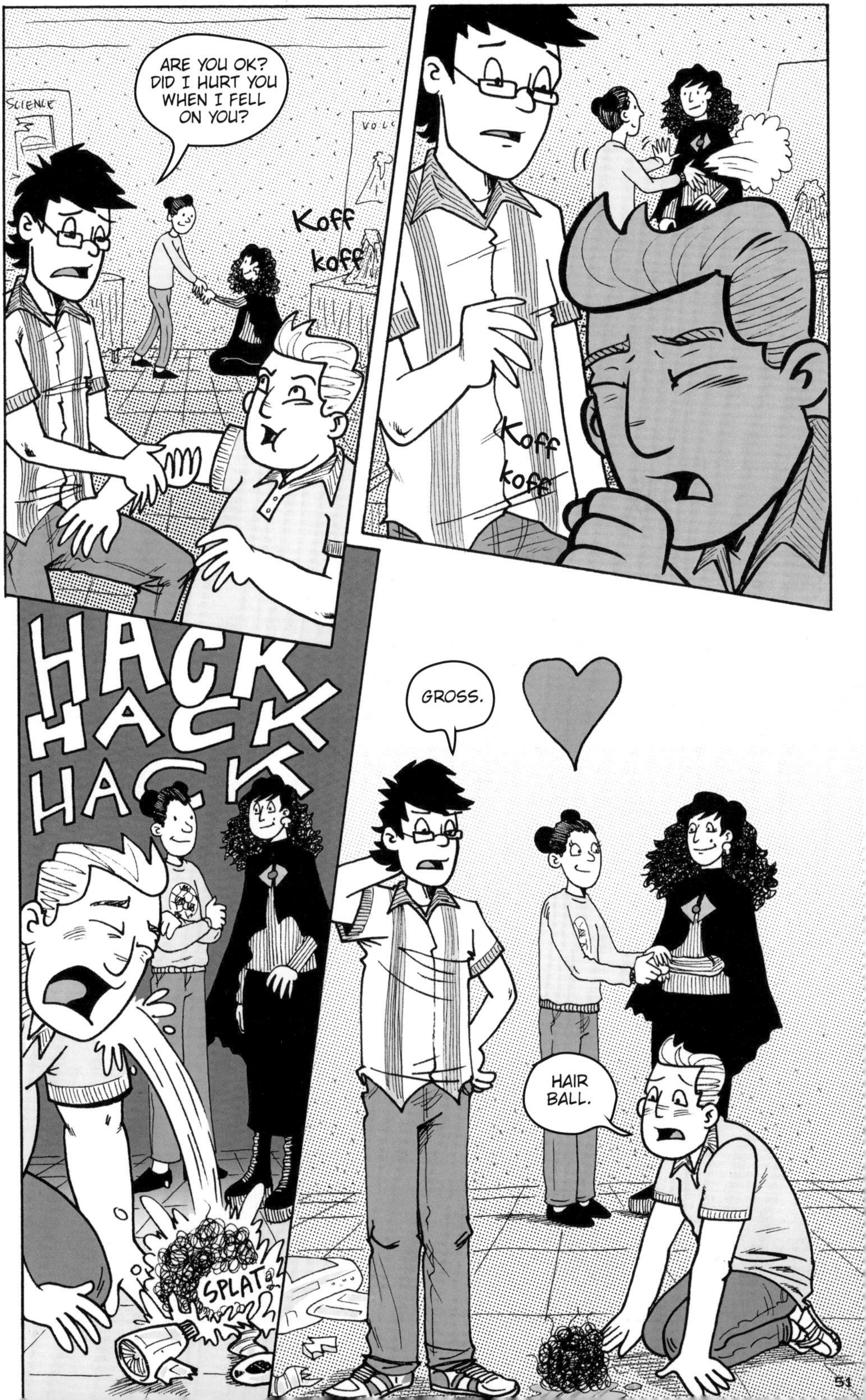
SCIENCE
ARE YOU OK? DID I HURT YOU WHEN I FELL ON YOU?
Koff koff
Koff koff
HACK HACK HACK
SPLAT
GROSS.
HAIR BALL.

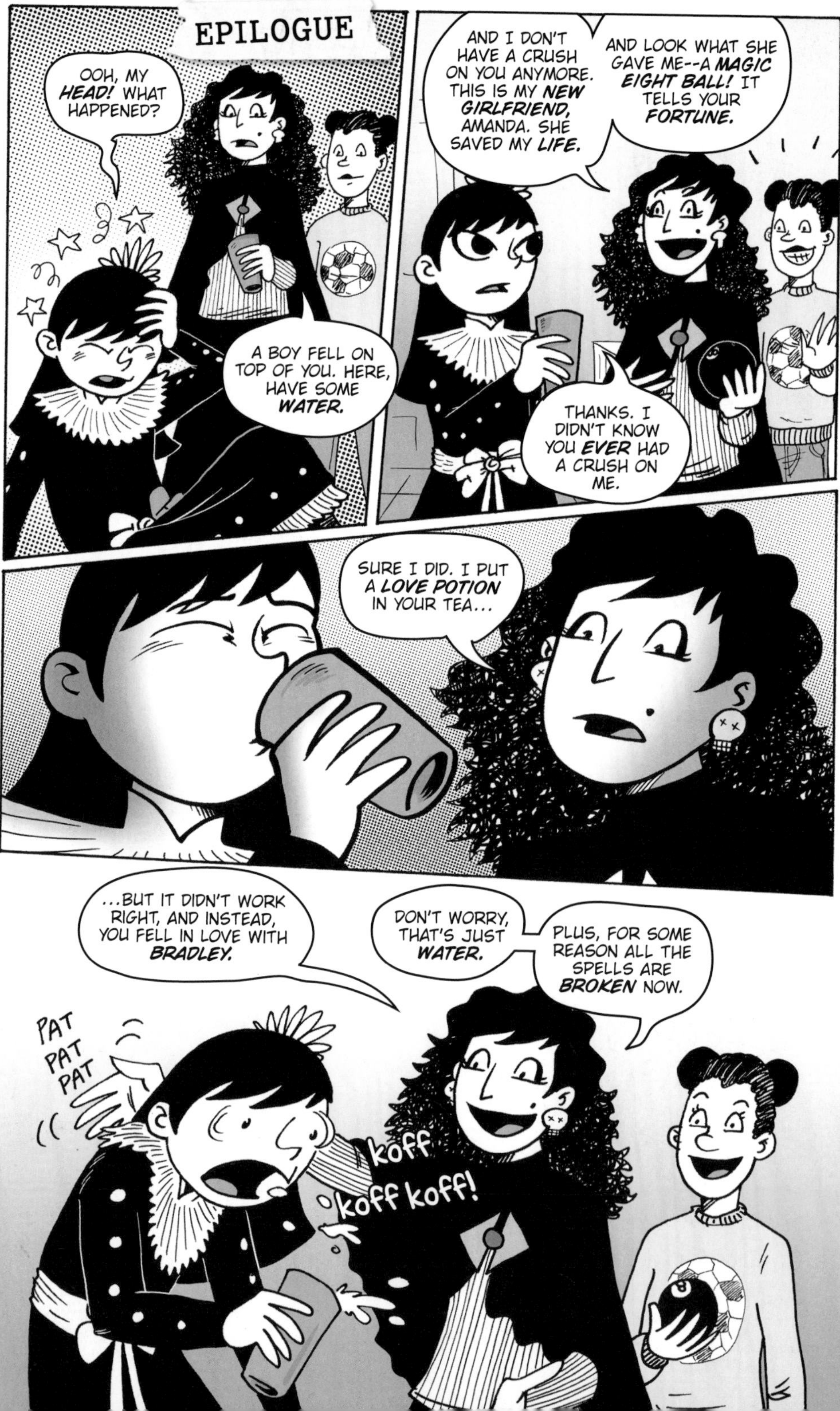
EPILOGUE
OOH, MY HEAD! WHAT HAPPENED?
A BOY FELL ON TOP OF YOU. HERE, HAVE SOME WATER.
AND I DON'T HAVE A CRUSH ON YOU ANYMORE. THIS IS MY NEW GIRLFRIEND, AMANDA. SHE SAVED MY LIFE.
AND LOOK WHAT SHE GAVE ME--A MAGIC EIGHT BALL! IT TELLS YOUR FORTUNE.
THANKS. I DIDN'T KNOW YOU EVER HAD A CRUSH ON ME.
SURE I DID. I PUT A LOVE POTION IN YOUR TEA...
...BUT IT DIDN'T WORK RIGHT, AND INSTEAD, YOU FELL IN LOVE WITH BRADLEY.
DON'T WORRY, THAT'S JUST WATER.
PLUS, FOR SOME REASON ALL THE SPELLS ARE BROKEN NOW.
PAT PAT PAT
koff
koff koff!

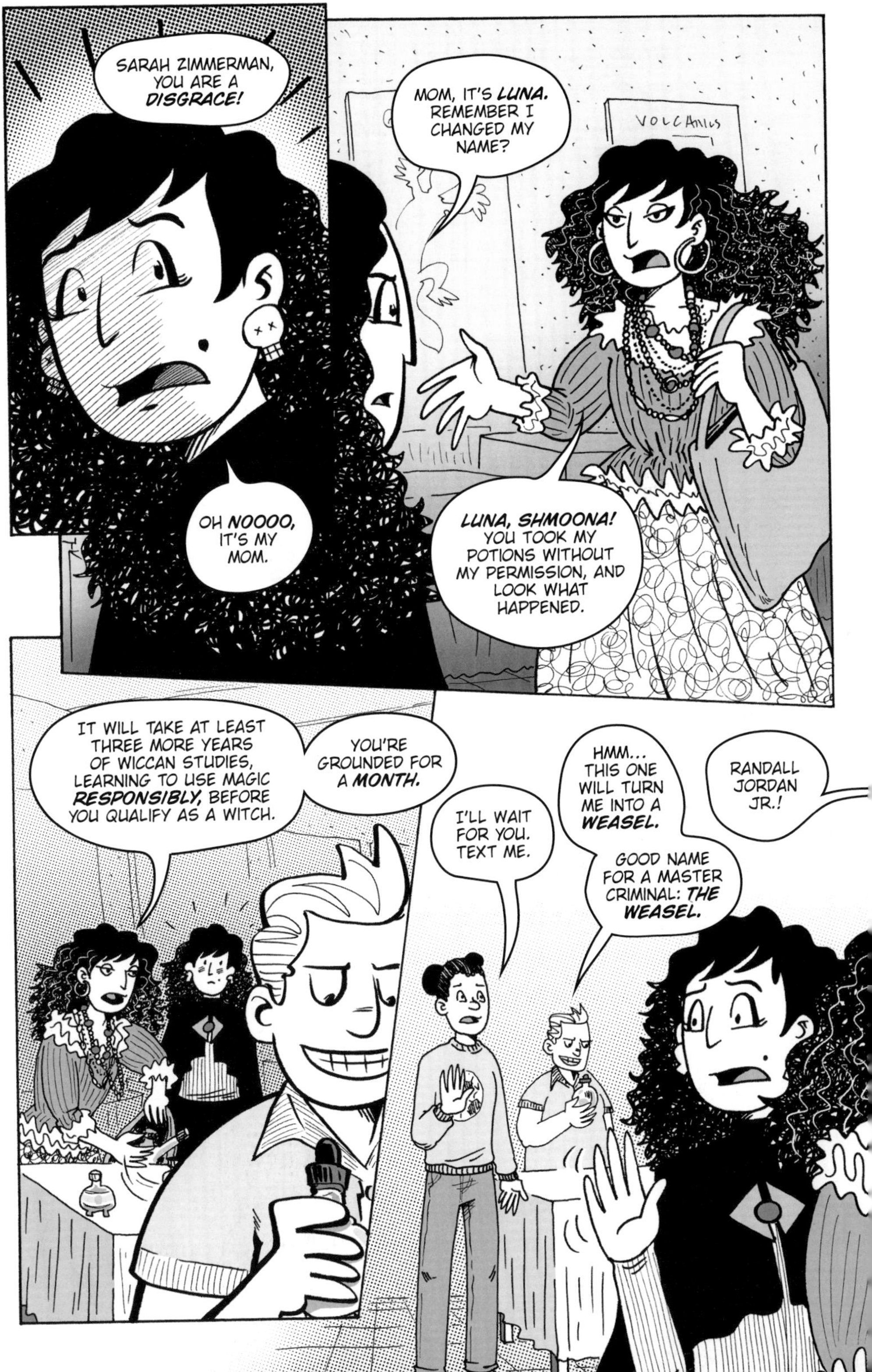
SARAH ZIMMERMAN, YOU ARE A DISGRACE!
MOM, IT'S LUNA. REMEMBER I CHANGED MY NAME?
VOLCANUS
OH NOOOO, IT'S MY MOM.
LUNA, SHMOONA! YOU TOOK MY POTIONS WITHOUT MY PERMISSION, AND LOOK WHAT HAPPENED.
IT WILL TAKE AT LEAST THREE MORE YEARS OF WICCAN STUDIES, LEARNING TO USE MAGIC RESPONSIBLY, BEFORE YOU QUALIFY AS A WITCH.
YOU'RE GROUNDED FOR A MONTH.
I'LL WAIT FOR YOU. TEXT ME.
HMM... THIS ONE WILL TURN ME INTO A WEASEL.
GOOD NAME FOR A MASTER CRIMINAL: THE WEASEL.
RANDALL JORDAN JR.!

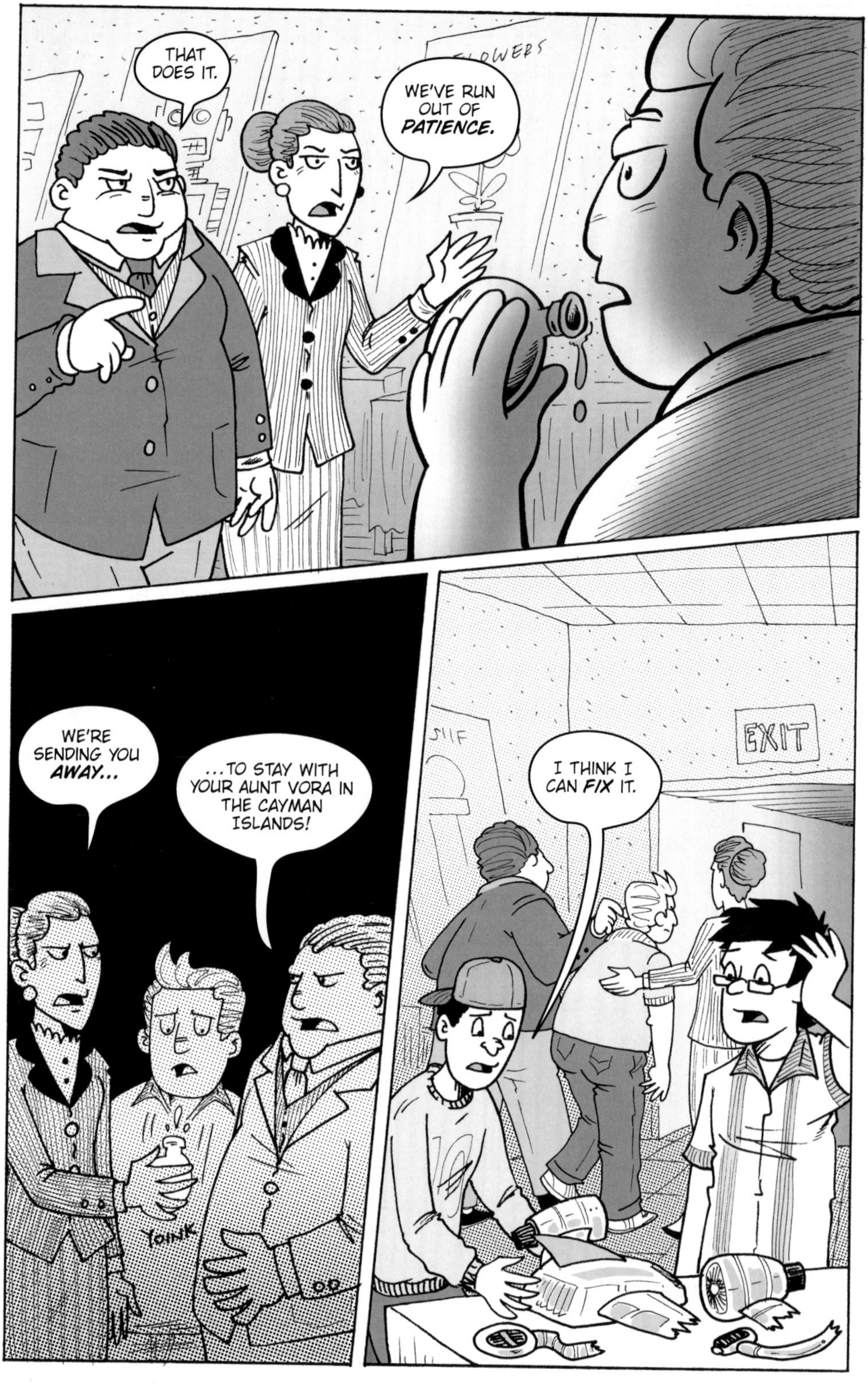
THAT DOES IT.
WE'VE RUN OUT OF PATIENCE.
WE'RE SENDING YOU AWAY...
...TO STAY WITH YOUR AUNT VORA IN THE CAYMAN ISLANDS!
YOINK
EXIT
I THINK I CAN FIX IT.

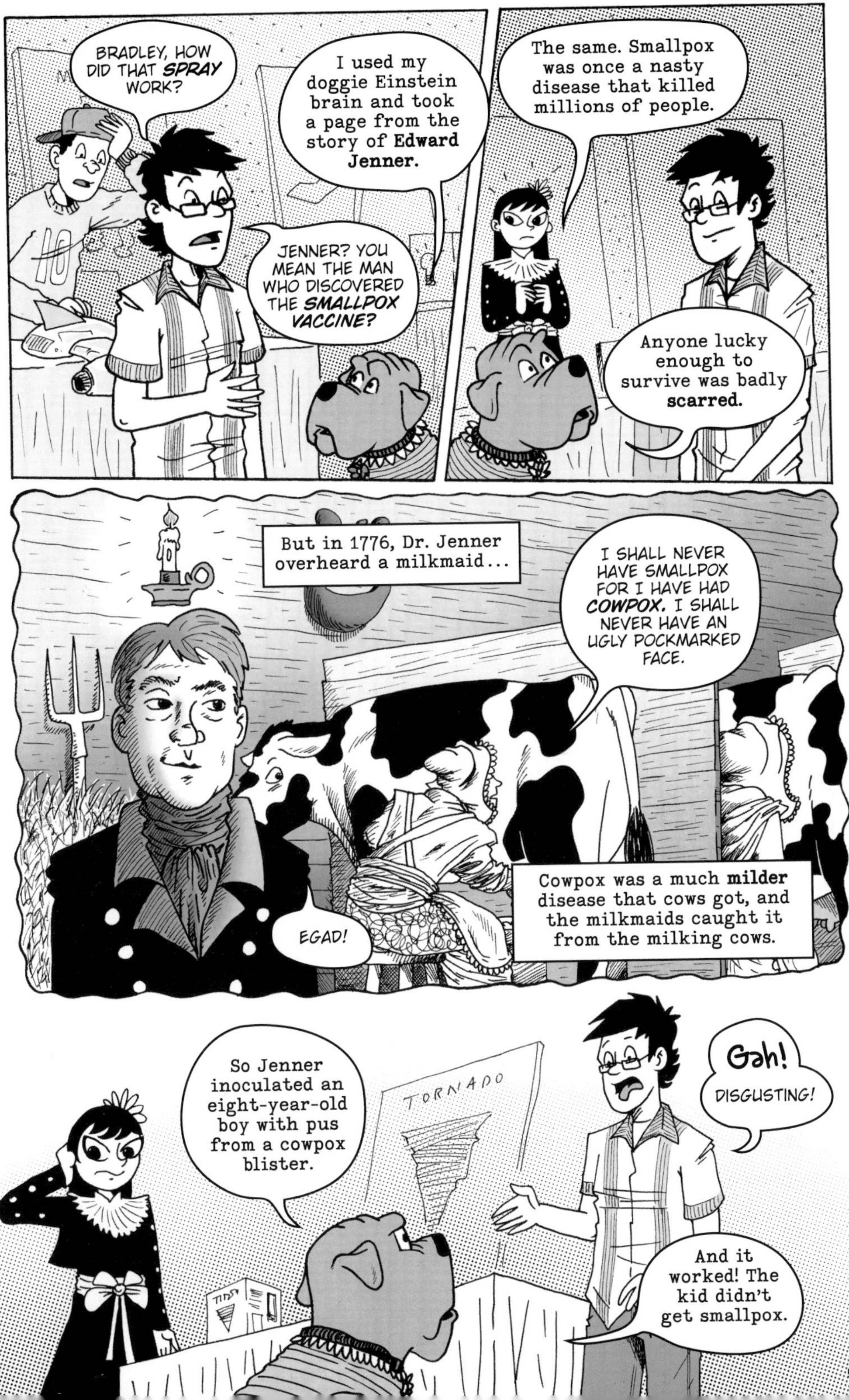
BRADLEY, HOW DID THAT SPRAY WORK?
I used my doggie Einstein brain and took a page from the story of Edward Jenner.
JENNER? YOU MEAN THE MAN WHO DISCOVERED THE SMALLPOX VACCINE?
The same. Smallpox was once a nasty disease that killed millions of people.
Anyone lucky enough to survive was badly scarred.
But in 1776, Dr. Jenner overheard a milkmaid...
I SHALL NEVER HAVE SMALLPOX FOR I HAVE HAD COWPOX. I SHALL NEVER HAVE AN UGLY POCKMARKED FACE.
EGAD!
Cowpox was a much milder disease that cows got, and the milkmaids caught it from the milking cows.
So Jenner inoculated an eight-year-old boy with pus from a cowpox blister.
TORNADO
Gah! DISGUSTING!
And it worked! The kid didn't get smallpox.

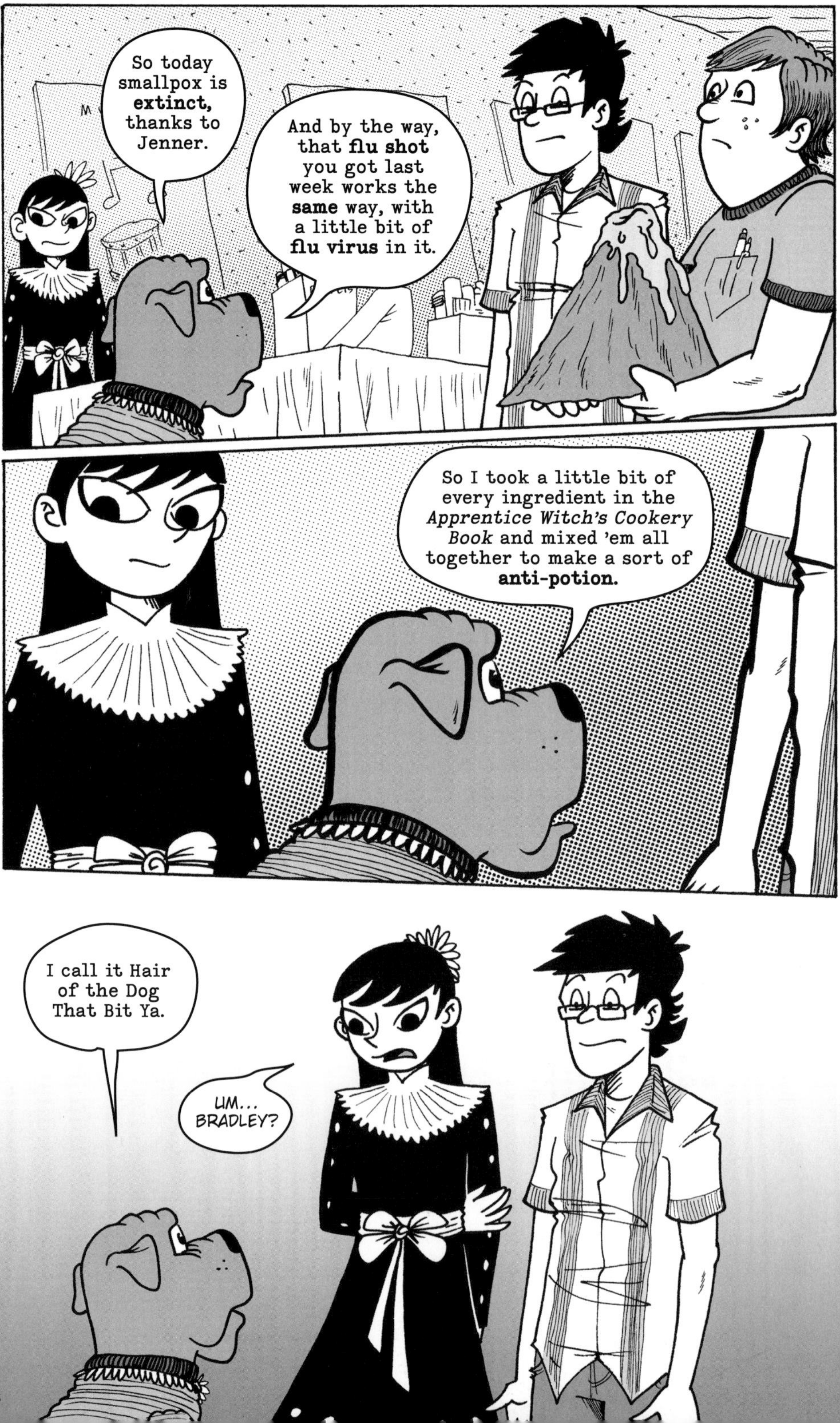
So today smallpox is **extinct,** thanks to Jenner.
And by the way, that **flu shot** you got last week works the **same** way, with a little bit of **flu virus** in it.
So I took a little bit of every ingredient in the *Apprentice Witch's Cookery Book* and mixed 'em all together to make a sort of **anti-potion.**
I call it Hair of the Dog That Bit Ya.
UM... BRADLEY?

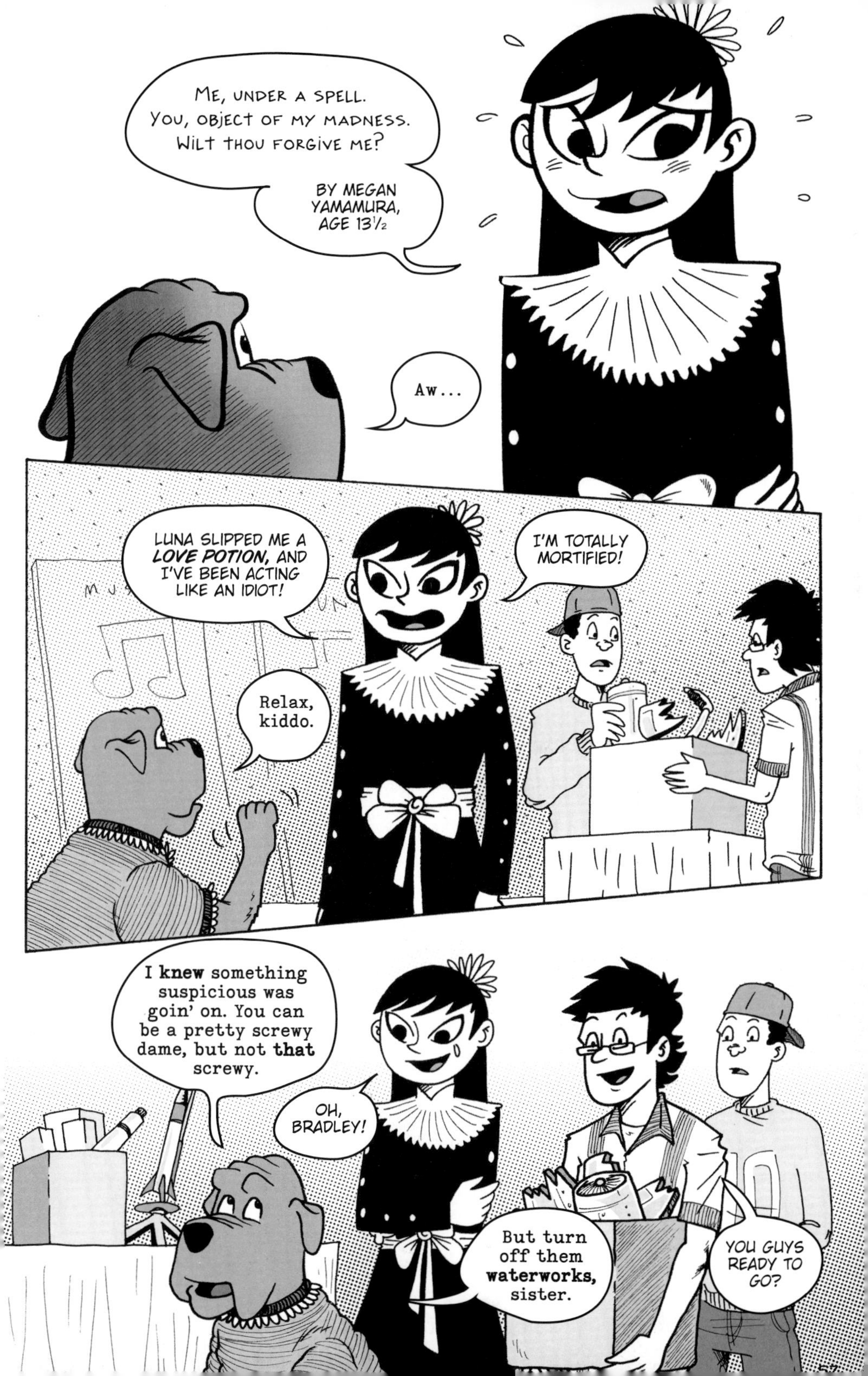
Me, under a spell.
You, object of my madness.
Wilt thou forgive me?
BY MEGAN YAMAMURA, AGE 13½
Aw...
LUNA SLIPPED ME A **LOVE POTION,** AND I'VE BEEN ACTING LIKE AN IDIOT!
I'M TOTALLY MORTIFIED!
Relax, kiddo.
I **knew** something suspicious was goin' on. You can be a pretty screwy dame, but not **that** screwy.
OH, BRADLEY!
But turn off them **waterworks,** sister.
YOU GUYS READY TO GO?

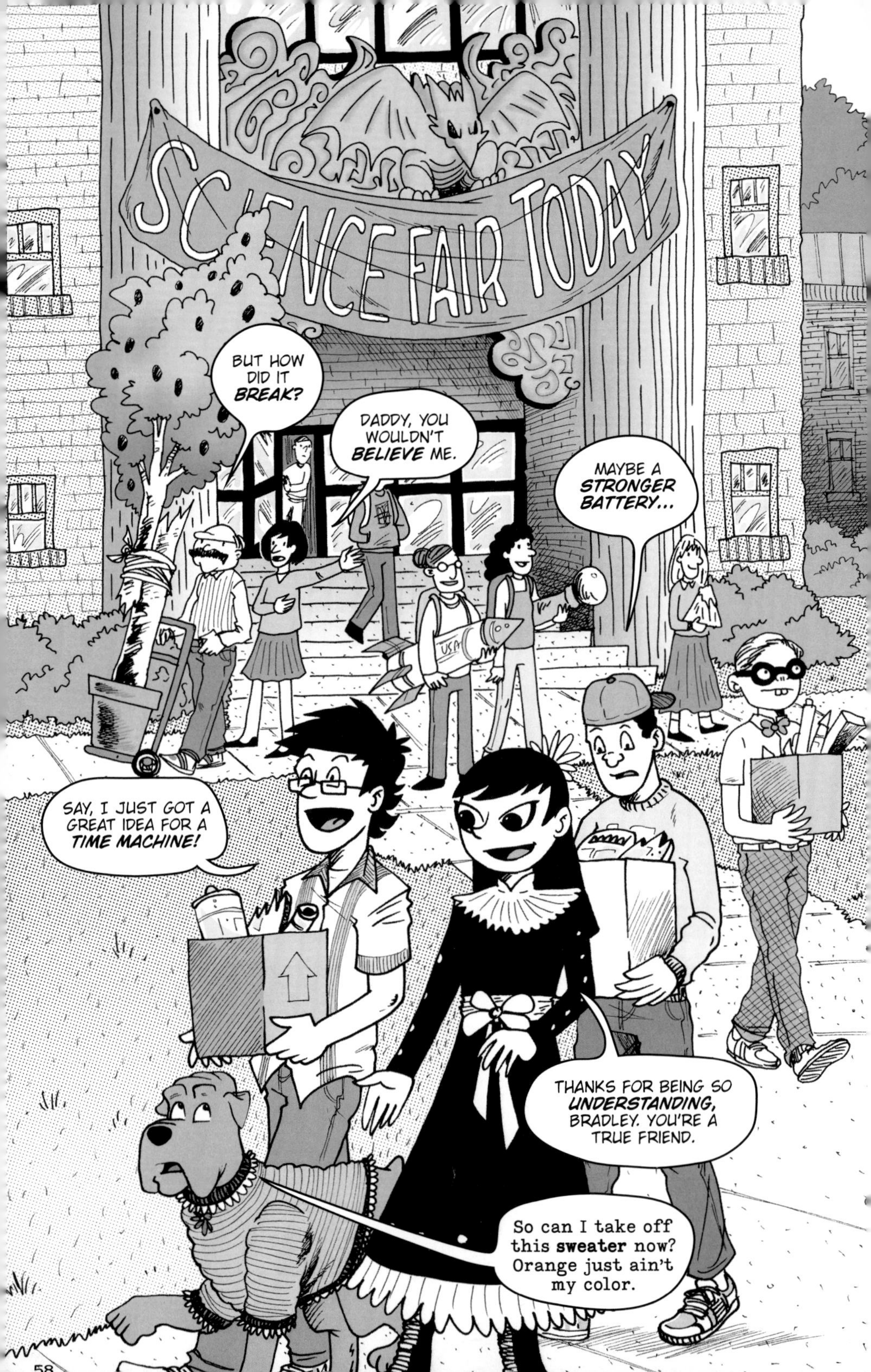
SCIENCE FAIR TODAY
BUT HOW DID IT BREAK?
DADDY, YOU WOULDN'T BELIEVE ME.
MAYBE A STRONGER BATTERY...
USA
SAY, I JUST GOT A GREAT IDEA FOR A TIME MACHINE!
THANKS FOR BEING SO UNDERSTANDING, BRADLEY. YOU'RE A TRUE FRIEND.
So can I take off this sweater now? Orange just ain't my color.

Login: chicagoland

Password: •••••••n|

Click here to interFACE

MYBLOGFACE

CHICAGOLAND DETECTIVE AGENCY

InforFACEtion

Location: Behind the counter of Hernandez & Sons Pet Supply store

Hours: 9–5 during summer vacation. During the rest of the year, after-school hours, except on weekends.

Proprietor: Raf Hernandez (that's me) because it's my mom's store

Our motto:
Sad? Scared? Need help fast?
Chicagoland Detectives:
We can do the job!

The Chicagoland Detective Agency is here for you. We solve low crimes and misdemeanors, and we battle injustice. Don't be afraid to come in with your pets. We love animals.

Friendly FACErs

38 Friends

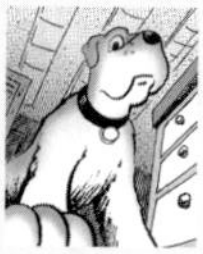

Bradley

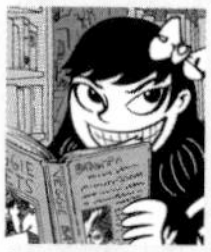

Megan Yamamura

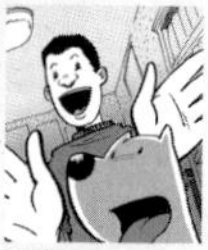

William Johnson

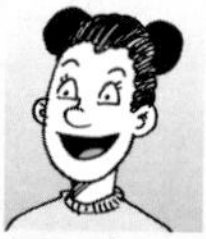

Amanda Jardine

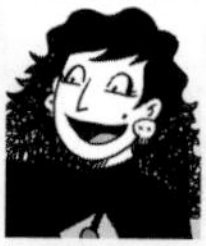

Luna Zimmerman

Chicagoland BLOG ENTRY #6

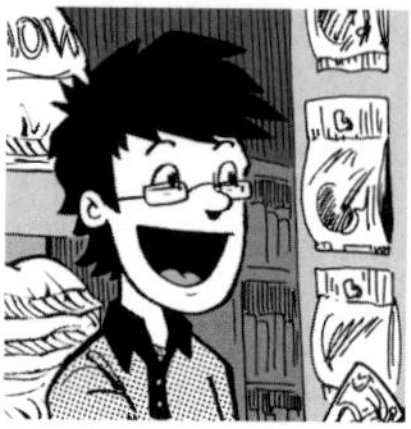

FIND IT AT THE LIBRARY!

By Raf Hernandez

For my last birthday, my mom gave me a gift card for that Internet auction site, HighEstate.net, but Bradley used up all the credit buying rare old reference books that we used to help solve our cases. So when I needed to get a book on spells and potions, instead of buying the book, I looked in our public library.

The library is amazing! They have books on every subject, more than anyone could ever read in their whole lifetime, and you can borrow them for free. But remember that you have to return the books in good condition and on time. Those overdue fees sure add up! So don't bend down the pages or underline words or anything! When Megan was mixing up that anti-potion witch's brew, I was afraid she'd splash it all over the book, but Bradley was careful not to get the book too close to the stove.

I'm a lucky kid. When I was five years old, my mom discovered that I was writing math problems on her computer, so she bought me one of my own. But not all kids are so lucky, and not all moms and dads can afford to buy a computer for their kids, so here's more good news about libraries: they have computers for kids (grown-ups too!) to use free.

So next time you need to do research or you just want something fun to read, find it at the library!

MYBLOGFACE

Meet the FACE

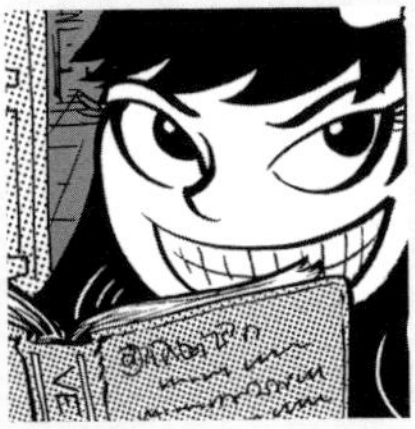

Megan Yamamura
Age: 13½
Education: Stepford Preparatory Academy
Profession: Detective

Guest Blogger: Megan Yamamura

I guess by now you know that witches are not crooked-nosed, warty, green women in pointy hats. And they're not devil worshippers either, but that's what people believed long ago. In 1692, four preteen girls caused a mass hysteria in Salem, Massachusetts, when they accused people of being witches and the villagers believed them. (I know, the villagers were as crazy as those girls!) By the time the craziness was over, nearly two hundred people, mostly women, had been accused of worshipping the devil, and twenty of them had been hanged. As for those girls who started it all, some people will do anything to get attention!

Anyway, having been a preteen girl myself just a year ago, I think those four girls in Salem were a disgrace to the name of preteen girls everywhere, so I have composed an angry haiku:

BAD GIRLS, SHAME ON YOU!
DISGRACING ALL PRETEEN GIRLS,
BAD GIRLS, YOU'RE GROUNDED!

Today most witches prefer to be called Wiccans, and if they worship anything, it's Earth and nature and animals, so they tend to be very nice people, like Luna. If you want to find out more about Wicca and Wiccans, you know where to go: the library!

Advertisement

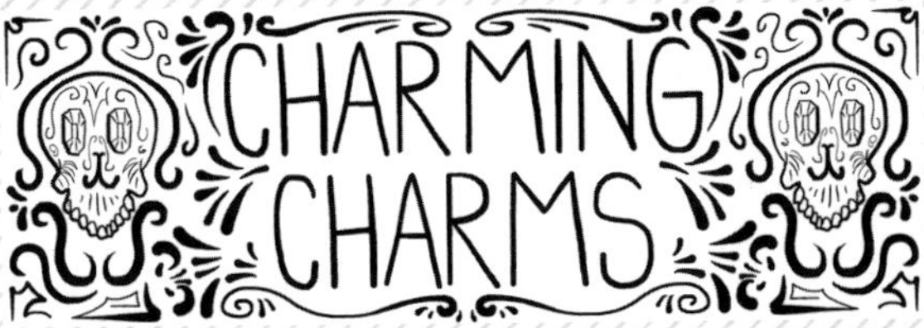
CHARMING
CHARMS

Advertisement

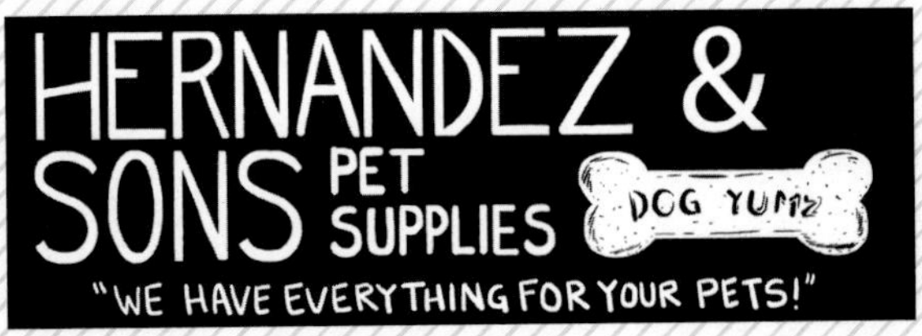
HERNANDEZ &
SONS PET SUPPLIES
DOG YUMZ
"WE HAVE EVERYTHING FOR YOUR PETS!"

Meet the FACE

Amanda Jardine
Age: 13
Education: James A. Garfield Middle School

Guest Blogger: Amanda Jardine

The Chicagoland Detective Agency totally rules! If not for you guys, I would never have had the courage to tell Luna how I felt about her or to give her the Magic Eight Ball I bought for her. (Of course, I then found out that real witches don't use stuff like Magic Eight Balls but whatever.)

Anyway, this whole experience has taught me something: If you really like somebody, you should tell them, instead of following them around like a lovesick puppy, like I did. Plus, following people around can get you in trouble. Look what happened to me: I almost got accused of a crime I didn't commit!

Meet the FACE

Luna Zimmerman
Age: 13
Education: James A. Garfield Middle School

Guest Blogger: Luna Zimmerman

The Chicagoland Detective Agency is awesome, and I want to thank them for solving the case of the missing potions, plus getting Amanda Jardine and me together.

But I'd also like to explain something: That Magic Eight Ball that Amanda gave me is just a fun toy, not real magic. If you've never seen one, it's a big black ball with a small transparent window on the bottom. The way it works is you hold it with the window away from you and ask it a question. Then you turn it toward you and see the answer float into the window. Some people shake it, but that just causes bubbles.

Even though we real witches never use toys like the Magic Eight Ball to read fortunes, it was very sweet of Amanda to give me one.

Advertisement

ABOUT THE AUTHOR AND ILLUSTRATOR

TRINA ROBBINS, an Eisner Award and Harvey Award nominee, made a name for herself in the underground comix movement of the 1960s. She published the first all-woman comic book in the 1970s; published her first history of women cartoonists, *Women and the Comics*, in the 1980s; was an artist for the *Wonder Woman* comic book; and created the superhero series *Go Girl!* with artist Anne Timmons. And that's just a start—she has written biographies, other nonfiction, and way too many other books and comics for kids and adults to list, but you can check them out on her website at www.trinarobbins.com. In 2013 she was voted into the Will Eisner Comic Book Hall of Fame. She lives in San Francisco with her partner, comics artist Steve Leialoha.

TYLER PAGE is an Eisner Award-nominated illustrator and webcomic artist who has self-published four graphic novels, including *Nothing Better*, recipient of a Xeric Foundation Grant. His day job is director of Print Technology at the Minneapolis College of Art and Design, where he oversees the college's print-based facilities. He's been drawing his whole life and sometime around middle school started making his own comics starring the family cat. He lives with wife Cori Doerrfeld, daughter Charlotte, and two crazy cats in Minneapolis, and his website lives at www.stylishvittles.com.